The
SEIZURE
of POWER

The
SEIZURE
of POWER

by
CZESLAW MILOSZ

CRITERION BOOKS, INC.   NEW YORK

C. 2

*Translated from the Polish by Celina Wieniewska
The quotations from Thucydides are given in the
translation of Richard Crawley*

To Jeanne

The fall of Warsaw and the
coming of Communist domination
are dramatized through episodes
in the lives of four Polish intellectuals.

AFTER A SHORT campaign in 1939, Poland, where the action of this novel takes place, was divided into two zones. The largest city in the German zone was Warsaw; in the Soviet zone, Lvov. Hitler's attack on Russia began on June 22, 1941, and led very quickly to the German occupation of the zone recently incorporated into the Soviet Union.

The Polish underground forces fighting the Nazis were known as the Home Army; they, together with the administrative apparatus of the underground state, were under the orders of the Polish *émigré* government in London. In addition to the Home Army, smaller groups of underground forces operated in Poland. The National Armed Forces were the instrument of the extreme right; the Home Army tried, with negligible results, to subordinate them to its orders. The People's Army, which was a Communist organization, did not recognize the authority of the London Polish government.

The great Red Army offensive halted on the line of the Vistula in the last days of July, 1944. On August 1 a rising against the Germans began in Warsaw. (The first rising, in the ghetto, had taken place in April, 1943.) Street-fighting in the city lasted over two months, until October 3. The insurgents were short of arms; and the Germans were able to encircle the various quarters of the city and reduce them one by one. The Old City was the first to surrender, on September 2, 1944.

After the failure of the rising, the population of Warsaw, numbering over one million, was deported. The Germans then destroyed by fire and explosives all the buildings which were still standing.

In the meantime, in the rear of the Red Army, a new Polish government, set up in Moscow and known at the time as the Committee of National Liberation, was already active in the town of Lublin. On January 17, 1945, the Red Army resumed its offensive, overran the ruins of Warsaw across the river (the Vistula separates Warsaw from its eastern suburb of Praga) and, in a rapid advance through Poland, marched toward Berlin.

The principal characters of this novel are fictitious, but some incidents of the fighting in the Old City are taken from an account by Roman Podlevski which has been published in Polish under the title: *Przemarsz Przez Pieklo* (The March Across Hell).

The
SEIZURE
of POWER

Part One

PROFESSOR GIL'S BREAKFAST *consisted of tea and bread: like many people who live alone he never remembered to buy butter or jam. Outside the windows, streetcars clattered past, their bent and bullet-riddled coaches rattling like tin cans; people were perched on the back buffers, clinging to others who had got a foothold on the edge of the platform. The wind carried clouds of red brick dust along the street. Professor Gil wondered how long it would take him to finish the chapter he was working on, and what the chances were that his efforts would not be wasted. But he knew that he should not depress himself by thinking about that: the small cards pinned to the wall, on which he had written out how much he must do each day, were an exercise in self-discipline, a refuge, a necessity, if not a hope.*

Thucydides was not much in favor at the moment. It would have been wiser to have chosen some other

3

Greek author for translation. If you selected your texts carefully, you could secure for yourself the position of a useful worker. The state that had deprived Gil, and others like him, of their university chairs, claiming that their influence on the young was bad, did not necessarily intend them to starve. The younger generation of professors had serious gaps in their education. For instance, none of the younger, politically loyal scholars knew Greek; and the state had its own reasons for publishing the classics—in small editions, it is true—proclaiming itself the heir to all previous civilization. The state publishing houses even handed out contracts for translations of old authors about whom there existed grave ideological doubts. This was disquieting: Professor Gil did not wish to live on state charity disguised as payment for work done. But Thucydides? Granted the edition would be a small one; yet wasn't the bitter futility of the massacres, ruses, stratagems, and struggles which crowded the pages of The Peloponnesian War *a dangerous image of history? The professor could remember the face of the director of the state publishing house at the moment of concluding the agreement. He was looking down, his eyes hidden by their lids; his benevolent, almost cordial smile an indefinable mixture of indulgence, bitterness, and irony.*

But there was an inner compensation in this choice of Thucydides—something like a belief that by preserving a relation with this Greek author, and even, under favorable circumstances, by giving him to a few young people to read, one justified oneself in some way; removed from oneself the stigma of being a

4

"survivor of nineteenth-century liberalism." This applied not only to Gil but also to Thucydides—although the things Thucydides witnessed were so vastly different from those that Gil was seeing.

At this hour the apartment was empty. The numerous subtenants who lodged in its five rooms had left early for offices in a more intact part of the city. Professor Gil took his empty glass to the kitchen and looked through the window into the dark courtyard where in the center, between the broken flagstones, a chestnut showed its first small green leaves. So many springs had gone by since the one which had brought the end of the war, the transfer of populations, an epidemic of typhus.

He put on a torn sweater and thought for a moment about replacing a missing button. But for this he would need thread: he must remember to ask his neighbor if she would like to exchange a spool of thread for a spare needle he still possessed. He spread his books on the table; they opened of their own accord at the right place; the pages bore the traces of his fingers. Then, in a small even hand, he began slowly to add sentence after sentence.

"Words had to change their ordinary meaning and to take that which was now given them. Reckless audacity came to be considered the courage of a loyal ally; prudent hesitation, specious cowardice; moderation was held to be a cloak for unmanliness; ability to see all sides of a question, inaptness to act on any. Frantic violence became the attribute of manliness; cautious plotting, a justifiable means of self-defence.

5

The advocate of extreme measures was always trust-worthy; his opponent a man to be suspected. To succeed in a plot was to have a shrewd head, to divine a plot a still shrewder; but to try to provide against having to do either was to break up your party and to be afraid of your adversaries. In fine, to forestall an intending criminal, or to suggest the idea of a crime where it was wanting, was equally commended, until even blood became a weaker tie than party, from the superior readiness of those united by the latter to dare everything without reserve; for such associations had not in view the blessings derivable from established institutions but were formed by ambition for their overthrow; and the confidence of their members in each other rested less on any religious sanction than upon complicity in crime."

SUMMER 1944

1

IT WAS JULY, 1944. Peter Kwinto, a political education officer of the First Polish Division, was strolling down a graveled walk strewn with yellow blossoms from the linden trees. He stopped where the row of trees came to an end and lush grass glistened in the sun. Red insects with black totem-like markings, coupled in their love rites, were swarming in a cleft between the roots of one of the trees. He stooped and watched them for a moment; then he straightened up and looked down the valley. As far as the eye could see, it was seething with activity. Unbroken columns of men and vehicles filled the roads and were spreading out across the hills on both sides of the river. Heavy tanks covered with leafy branches moved along in groups, the barrels of their guns rising and falling as they bumped over the uneven ground. Trucks packed with gray-uniformed soldiers; jeeps scurrying down rough side lanes; masses of Russian infantry pouring off the roads, marching in line across the brown fields of stubble and through the golden wheat; shouts, the blaring of horns, the roar of engines; great elongated clouds of dust, rising and forming into streaky layers over the agitated landscape.

He resumed his walk along the avenue in the shade of the ancient trees. On the lawn in front of the house some soldiers, their shirt sleeves rolled up, were butchering carcasses of hogs. Others were cleaning their rifles or, propped on their elbows and chewing blades of grass, lay on the ground in groups listening to instructors. A loudspeaker, probably being repaired, crackled and screeched, relaying snatches of a tune. Peter passed the white columns of the main entrance of the house and rounded the corner past the noisy kitchens full of smoke and the bustle of army cooks unloading loaves of bread and sides of meat from trucks. He entered the house through a side door. The unswept floor of the passage grated under his feet. He knocked at a door, unthinkingly stroking with his other hand a carving in the dark oak panel. During the German occupation the estate had been run by a control commission, the owners had been expelled, and only a female relative had been permitted to stay on. Peter had not yet seen her; she never appeared. All was silence behind the door. He knocked again. Now he could hear the shuffle of slippered feet, then silence again. Only after he had knocked a third time was the key turned in the lock and the door cautiously opened.

For a moment Peter and the woman stared at each other. Her fingers clutched at her housecoat—it was printed with large pink flowers—and held it tight around her neck. For a second her mouth twisted with fear and self-pity, then she managed a smile which was in obvious contrast to the red spots that appeared on her old face and the expression of her nervously darting eyes: "A real Bolshevik! Here, in front of me! What does he want?" Before he opened his mouth, Peter suddenly became conscious of the weight of the past five years. What he felt was a mixture of pity and revulsion; a disagreeable sensation that made him angry—and he could not say whether he was angry with himself for feeling the revulsion or because he found that he had pity to spare. He suddenly realized that from now on, in his native country, he would have to experience over and over again this state of suppressed irritation and that the present encounter was only the first of a long series, the sudden rediscovery of ties with a past he had thought dead.

"I'm sorry to disturb you, madame, but I've been told there's a library here. Would you be kind enough to show me where it is? This is a personal request," he added hastily, "I would like to borrow a book."

She managed to force a smile, a smile for conquerors.

"Yes, of course, by all means. But unfortunately," her face—by force of habit, Peter thought—took on an expression of tolerant superiority, "this is a library of French books. There are hardly any books in Polish," she hesitated, "or in Russian."

"It doesn't matter. I would like to see it all the same, if I may."

He followed her into the room, into a smell of old

11

furniture and something like incense. Blackened portraits of men in old-fashioned uniforms and in armor hung on the walls. The woman opened a second door and showed him large bookcases standing in semidarkness, their glass panes covered with cobwebs and dust. Peter tried unsuccessfully to open the first, and asked for a key. There was no key, but the next case opened with a screech when he pulled at the door; the locks were loose in their sockets and seemed bare and defenseless. He touched the backs of the books with pleasure: red leather with gold tooling. They reminded him of his childhood and the books in the house of his grandparents over which he had pored for hours on end, sitting on a settee covered with oilcloth, which gradually became warm from contact with his body. Most of all he had liked descriptions of travel in Africa and drawings in which naked Negroes paddled small rafts made of rushes or, leaning on their spears, stood by reed huts which looked like beaver lodges. The old lady watched him as he mounted a chair and took out volume after volume. The consciousness of being observed spoiled Peter's pleasure in reminiscence: the return to the old days, to the river by which he had built make-believe Negro huts, to the boat made from a hollowed-out tree trunk which he had pretended was a native canoe.

She thinks I've been sent here to confiscate the library, he thought. He glanced again at the volume he was holding in his hand and jumped down from the chair.

"I should like to borrow this book," he said. "I'll return it before we move on." He saw the tension recede from her face as she was seeing him to the door, still not sure that he would not turn back and demand a watch or some money.

He sat on the grass at the edge of the park, his back against a tree. The russet sun was veiled by clouds of dust churned up by the movement of wheels and the tramping of innumerable feet. It settled like white ash on the leaves. The air was thick with the fever of an army's advance. Aircraft roared high overhead, above the clouds. Out of the corner of his eye Peter watched for a moment a tank tilted clumsily to one side where it had halted on a slope near the village. Human figures were swarming around it. To have a tank break down was a favorite trick of the troops. Peter never knew how much they helped the engines to fail so that they could get separated from their units and enjoy for a while the pleasures of looting. He unbuttoned his tunic.

Paris seemed frozen forever as the book's illustrator had preserved it: artists in long blouses, midinettes knocking at a student's door, and the student, in tight trousers and long coat, yawning and stretching over his books; crinolined innocents planning how to cuckold their tradesmen husbands. The Paris in which he had lived just before 1939 seemed unreal to Peter; it merged with that Paris of horse omnibuses, secure in time, which was more tangible. That was probably why he had never been able to speak about Paris to Ivan. It had been in the Urals where both of them worked as woodcutters. Ivan was an illiterate peasant from the Carpathians. He had never been to a large town; and at night, when they lay on their hard wooden beds, he would ask questions, wanting precise answers. But Peter wished somehow to obliterate that whole period of his existence, for he could not accept it as a part of his history on which it was possible to look with detachment; he noticed that Paris had ceased to mean anything to him, that it was an unreal phase of his life which had to be destroyed if the new phase were to have any value at all.

The great pines of the Urals crashing to the earth; hands torn by the ax and bleeding; body covered with the bites of a microscopic fly that invaded the eyes, nose, and mouth in black swarms; the horror of winter; the search for rags to protect one's legs from frostbite; and the certainty of death: another year, then another, and it would all be over. It had not been necessary to destroy the past; it was crumbling of its own accord, and when he had thought about it he had merely shrugged his shoulders. Peter accepted what had happened to him as an inevitable punishment: punishment for having been a citizen of Herculaneum and Pompeii. Around him people had died slowly from malnutrition and scurvy, full of memories, praying and cursing. He had set his teeth and learned to be silent. After all, there was nothing to say. Things were as they were. Revenge was part of justice.

And now the advance of the Red Army—like lava, like a force of nature. And he, as part of this advance, was capable of understanding a little this grim force whose external appearance—or necessary manifestation—produced in most people terror and antlike agitation. Understanding—but is it enough to under-

14

stand? And that woman now, and millions of them, writhing helplessly in fear and hoping that the British . . . that the Americans . . . thinking they should bury their gold, that they should escape, should hide their dollars behind the wallpaper, should smile to cover their hatred. And the earth—violated, scarred by the barbed wire of concentration camps, soaked with blood, with the last cries of human beings and their ashes. It was the Europe of midinettes and of fat shopkeepers in nightcaps which had slowly brewed the poison that would kill it.

The bliss of being among the living, of feeling the sun on one's face. From the village below came the intermittent rattle of automatic weapons. Far away, beyond the horizon, the heavy breathing of artillery fire. Peter lifted his hand and moved his fingers, overcome with wonder at the year, the month, the day, and the hour.

2

DURING THE PAST few months when Peter's division was advancing westward—the nucleus of the new administration in the first of the countries to be conquered—he had been studying Winter's head: he knew by heart every contour and every wrinkle on it. A large skull, so closely clipped that it seemed almost bald; a square protruding jaw; narrow lips; short, slightly hooked nose, and small black eyes with a faintly apelike expression looking out alertly from folds of skin. And now, this Sunday morning, Peter had that face in front of him. Winter's jaws were working, chewing huge chunks of bread dipped in coffee. Flies were crawling on the table between them, collecting around the small pools of spilt coffee, their proboscises vibrating as they drank. The thought that soon perhaps a day would come when there would be no need to look at Winter any more was for Peter identical with the thought that one day the war would end. Although he accepted Winter's presence as he accepted disagreeable natural phenomena, it confused his mind when he tried to remember how everything had started.

In that already distant period, it was Winter who had been the immediate cause of Peter's arrest and of his journey to the Urals. As one of the people they trusted, he had prepared reports; and he had, of course, known Peter well, for at one time they had frequented the same Warsaw literary cafés. When Peter found himself in the Eastern zone in 1939, he did not quite know what to do. He contemplated escape across the Rumanian frontier; but on the basis of the most elementary sociological observations that plan did not seem very sensible: the limousines, fur coats, jewels, and Pekingese dogs which accompanied the exodus of the former government, after the German army had crushed the Polish forces, had a symbolic value. The return to power of that social class was impossible; such things never happened in history. A week of wandering along roads under fire from Messerschmidts was for Peter a week of reckoning, without his being actually aware of it. Consciously, he had felt nothing but exasperation and fury—but, in fact, he had experienced, too, the shame of complicity. Who was he to have written a doctoral dissertation on French poetry, to have watched ironically as the world moved towards disaster, to have benefited from grants which enabled him to live fairly comfortably in Warsaw or on the rue Monsieur-le-Prince? To escape? With people like that? Yet he was far from happy in the atmosphere of the Soviet occupation, and at last he decided to cross the frontier between the two zones and return to Nazi rule. At the time he refused to admit the reason to himself—a desire to be purified, to atone, to share the misfortunes of a humiliated people. He cherished, too, the completely irrational hope that from the chaos something new would emerge one day, something with a better, still undefined shape. But these motives were overshadowed by a great and, as it seemed to him, egotistical desire: to reorganize himself, to have plenty of time, to place himself somewhere outside official life where he could begin everything over again, where thought was free precisely because it was a completely clandestine activity, because it was entirely prohibited.

His arrest came at the moment of this decision: at dawn, in accordance with all the known rules of the game. At the end of a few weeks he received his sentence: five years for counterrevolutionary activities. Winter, who had denounced him, was right after all. He had belonged to a caste which was expendable. Before the war, Winter had spent a few years in prison as a Communist. He was fanatical and full of bitterness: moreover, he too was afraid of the Russians. And, as a matter of fact, Peter really was the author of the article which formed the basis of the charge against him. He had spoken maliciously in it about Communist poets and their intellectual dishonesty. Had it not been for the amnesty, Winter would probably have been guilty of his death. When Peter returned from Asia, after the others, to join the division, he found Winter there already, and everything had to be forgotten. They shook hands: Winter's small eyes were cold, hard, and alert.

Around them at other tables, men in clumsy uniforms were finishing breakfast and chatting; the air was full of cigarette smoke. Through the window came the light of a bright morning, the cries of swallows, the whistling and laughter of soldiers. Winter wiped his mouth, looked at his watch, and pulled down his tunic.

"Shall we go?" he asked.

"The priest won't start without us. He knows."

"It doesn't matter. We have to show him that we're punctual."

The battalion was marching out through the park gateway whose wrought-iron gates had been torn down and thrown in the nettles. The road ran downhill; its dust covered their boots. Peter looked at the small straw-thatched cottages with their tall sunflowers and hollyhocks. My country. Everything on a small scale, clutching at bits of land—small fields, small gardens, narrow boundary strips, a peasant with his only horse, an old woman with her cow, an inn, a village shop, neighbors leaning against fences, small girls with bare

18

red feet driving geese—a world innocent of mechanized warfare and books on political theory.

The battalion was singing a lively folk song. People, in their Sunday clothes, stood in the village street, open-mouthed and wide-eyed, watching the Polish troops, the same familiar uniforms, the same song. Soviet soldiers, unsmiling and a little scornful, leaned against their big tanks and looked at the marching men in their clean new uniforms. What did the peasants think? Their land had been crushed by tanks built in the Ruhr; they had known terror and man hunts and blue-eyed, fair-haired children taken from their mothers by force so that the Nordic strain might be strengthened in the Reich. Now at last they saw tanks built beyond the Urals. Everything reached them from the outside: a punishment, a calamity, the edge of a cyclone whose center was always somewhere else, somewhere far away in an unknown country or in the minds of unknown people.

On the green in front of the little wooden church the brightly colored kerchiefs of the women mingled with the black caps of the men. Garlands of leaves and wilted flowers hung above the open door. Now the first rank of soldiers went in. Peter, turning his head, saw the faces of those who had remained at the entrance—a mass of soldierly, close-cropped heads, and the mustached, wrinkled faces of the peasants. Like him, these soldiers had been deported once to the wide spaces of Asia, to camps on the shores of the Arctic Ocean, to die there of hunger and scurvy. They were aware of so much. Did they feel that they were

19

taking part in a masquerade, that their presence here, in the village church, by the will of the Russian command, was a practical joke played by destiny? At any rate they were happy. After all that, after the despair and the boundless vastness of a continent, they were back again; once again, as in their childhood, they could breathe the odor of old timber, of flowers and incense; they could take part in a communal rite which existed unquestioned and which to the senses was the strongest affirmation of their native land.

Small boys in surplices tinkled little bells. The sound of the organ, the chasuble of the priest, old peasant women moving their fingers along the large print of their prayer books. Peter thought of the graves of Soviet soldiers. There were hundreds of thousands of those graves between the Volga and the Vistula. They were marked with small wooden pyramids bearing the Red Star. He did not know why this emblem was so infinitely sad. Perhaps it was only a habit of the imagination, and perhaps because the cross was the simplest two-dimensional form to be found in nature—the form of man, the form of a tree. The tombs of Soviet soldiers imitated marble mausoleums, and the boards of which they were made were clumsily painted to imitate stone. To rest under this symbol of the new religion which, to commemorate individual death, could create only a diminutive copy of the pyramids, those memorials erected to the glory of empires and kings? He felt a pang when he looked at those graves. Perhaps it was because he held a grudge against a state which left not even its dead in peace, which did not permit them to lie under any sign which was not a sign of its power?

The small sun of the monstrance. I am probably thinking what they are all thinking, Peter said to himself. That I am alive. Though I've had a hard time and have ceased to be what I used to be, I must not forget the common lot of men and must not demand a different lot for myself. I must find again the way to justice. I must reject in myself and in every other human being what is superfluous and preserve only what is worth keeping. I must make the right use of my anger. I must find in myself the strength which comes from silence.

Winter stood next to him, his head bowed. The son of a Jewish bookbinder from the Warsaw ghetto, he considered his presence here to be useful, therefore necessary, therefore rational; he was the spiritual heir of passionate atheists who had not yet understood that religion can be a political weapon like any other. In spite of himself, Peter felt a grudging sympathy for Winter because he knew of his inexorable secret suffering. Winter would never find his parents. Peter's mother might not be alive either, but what Winter had before him were ruins and the ashes of crematoria, and not even a glimmer of hope. And behind him he had the death of his child. From half-spoken words uttered during those months Peter could guess that the year Winter had spent at Ashabad had not been much easier for him than the months in prisons and labor camps had been for himself. His child had lain dying on the mud floor of a Turkmen hut and he could do

21

nothing, not even blaspheme against God and the state. He had to accept the absurd and not even call it by its proper name. Like the old Turkmen with their yellow, crumpled faces, he could only look into the pitiless, burning sun and accept malaria, penury, and oppression as inevitable. Peter had learned resignation, but he thought it was probably a different kind than Winter's. It was rather prudence, an instinct. He felt it in himself as a temporary condition, like the relaxing of muscular tension in an animal falling from a height. And it seemed to him that he was happier than Winter. Even if it was only an illusion, it helped him to get rid of his dislike—until the time came when he didn't have to see Winter any more. At this moment he was almost ready to extend his hand and touch Winter's as a sign of brotherhood.

They went out into the glaring light. Soviet soldiers sitting on the churchyard wall were staring at a sight which must have seemed incomparably exotic to them —Polish soldiers mixing with the local people, joking and making the girls giggle. Suddenly Peter heard a scream. Before he could realize where this high-pitched, penetrating cry had come from, something warm, a bundle of gestures and wailing, threw itself at his feet and, reaching up from below, embraced his waist. The woman's shawl had slipped back from her head and her hair was disheveled. She had blank, imploring eyes, an open mouth: "Jesus, O Jesus, they took him! Help me, sir! They took my son away!" She was clutching Peter's uniform. "Sir, you're a Pole, it's not possible, he's innocent, he fought the Germans!"

22

Peter pushed her hands away. "Help me, save me! You're Poles too! The NKVD took my son away. Why? What for?" Peter saw his men gathering around him. They lowered their eyes, their mouths were grave. "I can't do anything. This isn't our affair." Winter appeared next to them. He said:

"Stop crying, woman. This is war, the front's here. They'll check up on him and let him go."

He ordered the men to fall in.

"Damn all this business," he said to Peter, "but it can't be helped. They're cleaning up this district. It's a bad mess even though the only partisan groups around here were under the London fascists. In fact, all the youngsters in these parts were in the Home Army."

3

"GENTLY, GENTLY. FOR us, words are the greatest danger. We must learn another language. It is difficult even to tell a story. You know that yourself. And besides, I don't propose to hide my hatred."

That was Julian. To have him facing you, thought Peter, was as inconceivable as to have before you a figure resurrected from the pages of history. To his friend, Julian had been part of a great crowd of shadows—and yet here he was, his eyes screwed up as in the past, with the same malicious laugh still shining in them.

"Of course, I could have left the ghetto earlier. Michael wanted to take me to his place. And Michael was well off. He was trading in flour. But his dear little soul was a bit dirty. A humanitarian, dirty little soul. I could see how scared he was. And his wife was even more frightened. For his sake. That sense of duty. Just like when that bastard Tom got me fired from my lectureship and some people protested because they felt ashamed that a Jew was being shown the door. Shame—the struggle between one form of cowardice and another. I preferred to stay on in the ghetto."

"You prefer that people should have no cowardice to overcome? Not to feel cowardly at all?"

"Yes. That's what I *would* like. Besides, it was better like that. I was earning my living in the ghetto by giving lessons. All the young people were studying. I've never seen people study so much: English, French, Spanish, Hebrew—even Latin and Greek. Many vocabularies and much grammar went up to heaven in the flames. But it did help one to remain alive over there in the ghetto. How can a person memorizing grammar admit to himself that there's no hope?"

Julian leaned his elbows on the sticky table top. His black coat was shiny with wear and very dirty. Under it he wore a Soviet military blouse. His thin face was covered with a dark stubble.

"All the same, I wanted to save my skin. In 1942 everything was clear. I was attached to a brigade that was driven to work in the city every day, and we got a plan worked out. One evening we bribed the drivers to take us to the very end of Independence Avenue —into the fields—instead of back to the ghetto. Four truckloads. It was September. You don't know what

24

a Jewish slave worker looked like: two canvas bags over his shoulder with all his possession inside, and if he could manage it, another sack on his back. Those who escaped were leaving their families to face certain death. I left my parents behind. I told them beforehand I would try to escape."

A waitress put some coffee in front of them. Loose bracelets jangled on her slim arms. Women of the intelligentsia impoverished by the war were new to Peter. He realized that the look he gave her was disagreeable: as if she were an exotic fish in a tank. She moved from the table swaying her hips slightly, elegant, upright, balancing her tray. Julian did not spare her a look. He was stirring his coffee with concentration.

"Now, of course, I'm well known as a guerrilla of the People's Army. All right, let's call it luck. But today luck isn't accidental."

"Julian! You in the forest! That's really very funny."

"Naturally I was badly prepared for life in the forest. When we left Warsaw we were going south, intending to turn back and go eastward later. That was the only feasible plan—the Red partisans were all in the east. And the Home Army didn't take Jews."

"Didn't it?"

"It didn't. We only marched at night. Five of us. Three men and two girls. Then we were ambushed by the National Armed Forces. Michael in Warsaw was the noble theorist of that noble movement. Nationalism, tradition, Catholicism, the struggle against the Germans, and all that. He published his nonsense in their underground papers. But in practice their units

25

concentrated on ridding the country of Jews and Communists, who for them, as you know, amount to the same thing. The attack drove us out of the forest into the fields, where German police were waiting. They caught the four others and killed them, but I saw a little pond and jumped in and lay among the reeds with my mouth just out of the water."

That was how they had had to learn reality. Peter remembered their discussions on phenomenology, late at night, in a small café near the university. He smiled and said:

"People used to call you Julian the Apostate."

"That didn't help me much. I don't know how I've managed to survive. I found myself completely alone. I was afraid to approach villages. While I had the strength I moved about only at night. At last I lay down to die. I was so hungry and weak that it seemed the easiest way out. I just dozed off. A gentle transition."

Was it really necessary for all this to have happened? Would the experience bring purification? Or the opposite? Peter looked at Julian as if trying to read in his face a clue which would help him understand himself. Julian went on with his story:

"Then it happened—just like something in a historical novel. I was saved by Jews from the forest. They found me and took me to their 'bunker.' It was terribly overcrowded. A whole family lived there: an old man with a prophet's beard, and his son with his wife and three children—all of them in a hole dug in the clay, covered with a roof of planks. On top there was a thick layer of earth with some shrubs planted

26

in it. Even if somebody had stumbled on the place he wouldn't have suspected that there were people living inside."

"And they, weren't they afraid? Can you understand why they took you in?"

"Afraid? That's much too weak a word. They hardly had enough room for themselves. I had to listen to their quarrels as if I were some inanimate object. The woman was always nagging at them for the folly they'd committed by taking me in. The old man said it had had to be done. The son explained that it was better this way, for I might have been found in the forest by somebody else, who might have started searching around then and causing trouble. Those people didn't conceal their fear. They weren't ashamed of it."

Peter sensed on his back the looks of women and men whispering with each other at the neighboring tables. The enmity between these people and those wearing Soviet or Polish uniforms was almost tangible.

"Those Jews came from a neighboring village," Julian continued. "They used to have a little shop there. Every two or three days, the son would go to the village at night to see his farmer friends and get food. He had some arrangement with them. Winter time was the worst—tracks could be seen in the snow. When I joined them they had been in their hole for a year. They tried to store up provisions so as not to have to go out at all in the winter. To have one person more to feed upset their calculations."

"Snow is treacherous stuff," said Peter, stirring the grounds of ersatz coffee in his cup. "I know something about it."

"I stayed with them for a month. Then the son learned from the peasants that a unit of Red partisans had been seen in the forest not far away. Escaped Soviet prisoners, Jews, different people from the towns: a mixed lot, thrown together by chance, of course. I didn't know whether the man was telling the truth or whether they simply wanted to get rid of me. But off I went. They gave me some food and showed me the way. And I found that unit. They treated me with great respect. I was an intellectual, you see. I edited a paper for them which was run off on a duplicator."

Peter wanted to say something about old Julian Halpern, the enemy of Hegel, but it seemed nonsense to him even before he had said it. So he simply remarked, as if making an observation about the weather:

"So here we are on this side. We'll be in Warsaw soon."

"People here and people there," Julian made a circle with his hand, "do you realize what they think? Here, in this town which isn't far from Maidanek where thousands of pairs of eyeglasses and toothbrushes and toys are lying in piles. Each toy means that a child has been killed. And people think that, all the same, some good has come out of it because there aren't any Jews left."

"Yes. It's not my job to defend them. But you ought to know what happened in the Ukraine. In the Soviet Ukraine. When the Germans came, not a single Jew escaped. Nobody had a chance. The non-Jewish Ukrainians betrayed them all. Which, incidentally, is only a technical remark: where no private property exists, a human being is at the mercy of the collective. And the collective was getting rid of its Jews."

"Do you understand the forces behind all this?'

"I understand that things can't be otherwise."

Julian roared:

"These pompous curs. They'll stay on in England, and as the years pass, they'll be corroded completely by their own lies. They'll publish two papers opposing each other: 'The London Bee' and 'The Scottish Wasp.' That's what they'll do to their dying day."

"There was something said once about a brave new world."

"Of course, I remember. No one can choose the time he's born in. Nor its morals. Nor, however much he hates airplanes, can he travel by stagecoach."

4

THE EDITORIAL OFFICES of the *New Era* occupied the same premises the Germans had used a short time before to publish their propaganda paper. The floor was littered with straw on which all the members of the staff slept at night. In every corner stood sacks of food which Baruga, the editor, had succeeded in acquiring for the canteen.

Baruga, in an unbuttoned shirt, his military trousers tucked into heavy Russian boots, was fighting a losing battle with the telephone—banging the receiver down with rage, then redoubling his efforts. His eyelids were red, his face swollen from lack of sleep. He was swearing horribly, and in his purring voice the oaths sounded incongruous.

"The fools," he shouted. "The fools! I told them to send a car. We need these people. Bastards! Now they're playing around at arresting people when we need them here to work."

He threw down the telephone receiver again and straightened his clumsy body.

"Gajevicz, you have to go right now and see this creature Pekielski. A mi-ni-ster, damn his eyes. See this damned nincompoop of a mi-ni-ster and tell him to get these people released at once."

"Where the hell are those damned pamphlets?" he roared. "The army's on the Vistula already. Warsaw is going to be liberated today or tomorrow, and how will we look? I'll wring the necks of those goddamned printers unless they learn to work. I'll wring their necks, but I'll teach them!"

Peter Kwinto, sweating in the heat, was hurriedly writing an article. At the table next to him, Julian Halpern, with earphones on his head, was jotting down communiqués.

Peter thought of his assignment to the newspaper as entry into a new world—a better one for him at the time: the feverish work, Baruga shouting, days mixed up with nights, articles, proofs, the smell of printer's ink. Moreover, Winter had remained in the army and disappeared from his field of vision.

The article he was writing was a commentary on the manifesto issued by the new government that was moving westward with the Red Army. The situation of 1920—when three Polish revolutionaries, Dzier-zynski, Marchlevski, and Kon, had been ready to take over power in Warsaw and were addressing manifes-toes to the nation—was being repeated. But, thought Peter, revolutionary situations improve little by little. After these two dozen years the troops who were bringing the new order were no longer a horde of badly equipped, undisciplined rebels. And during these same years the nationalism which might have opposed this new order had withered away like the dead branch of a tree. It was the Nazis who had reduced what was left of this nationalism to an absurdity. Besides, there had been an enormous improvement in the technique of revolution.

"Jam, what people want is jam," Baruga was fond of saying. The consciousness of history advancing by stages. "Over how many years will these stages of the revolution be spread?" Peter was wondering, while writing that the land reform proclaimed by the new government would respect the private property of the peasants. Yes, it was necessary to say this, for nobody wanted a bloody overturn. The revolution would be peaceful. New social forms would arise; they would not be the same as in Russia, nor like those under capitalism. A different, completely new road led toward socialism. And those who, like Peter's soldiers, sup-pressed their hatred of what they had seen in the East, must be encouraged to dedicate themselves to the good of their country and, with a clear conscience, to cheer the national flag.

It was this nationalistic flavor with which every sen-tence had to be seasoned that Peter found particularly

31

disagreeable. Before the war, the jingoism of the professional patriots had been a pet object of derision among all intellectuals. Baruga, in those days one of the editors of a crypto-Communist paper, went all out in ridiculing their slogans and thus won the recognition of a "thinking" public. Now the same slogans were being revived and given a new interpretation. "Beat the Germans, kill them, don't spare any woman or child, fertilize the earth with the enemy's blood, fight for the greatness and independence of the nation" —exhortations like these were repeated incessantly. And those broadcast appeals directed to the far side of the Vistula: "Rise up! Fire on the Germans. Cut off their escape! Take up arms, the hour of revenge has come!" Peter experienced a certain difficulty in using these words. A personal difficulty, for such words seemed to come to others in ready-made formulas, smoothed down by constant usage like a rifle butt. It was a question of upbringing, of training. But he, each time, had to weigh them up again, reassemble them, and be astonished at his work and its outcome. The words, when subjected to careful scrutiny, disclosed the utterly conventional character of the current phrases which served for the exchange of feelings. Whole sentences were used now in place of the few sounds which primitive man had found adequate to express sympathy or dislike. All the same, Valéry was somewhat more precise. Yet one could do nothing. These elementary sounds were a part of reality; perhaps by the very fact of crossing out those words that seemed overused he was giving his sentences a greater force than was necessary.

32

He inserted a full stop and stretched himself. Baruga was making a fuss again at his table, this time scolding someone for careless proofreading.

It was then that it happened. Julian screamed, "Be quiet!," silencing the arguments and the clatter of typewriters. They looked at him as with both hands he pressed the earphones against his head. He raised his eyes. They were not screwed up as usual, but seemed full of tension and interest. He looked steadily around and seemed to be waiting for an answer before he opened his mouth:

"A rising has broken out in Warsaw. The Londoners are playing their last card."

Baruga sat leaning forward, immobile. His face took on the sad, doglike expression that it always wore when he was silent and pensive. He reached for a cigarette and turned it in his fingers. From his throat came a loud grunt. He lit the cigarette and leaned on his elbows: "So," he said, "so."

Julian screwed up his eyes again—they reflected now the light of an inner explosion. The girls at the typewriters were gaping openmouthed, obviously uncertain what feelings they ought to show and how they should behave. Somebody was breathing on his eyeglasses, rubbing the lenses, and then looking at them against the light. The street rang with the songs of Soviet soldiers. Peter put the pages of his article in the correct order, put an ashtray on them and, trying to make as much noise as possible, got up, scraping his chair on the floor.

5

THE PLAIN WAS completely flat, merging in a straight line with the sky. A gray plain—fields of stubble, yellowish sandy soil, the uncertain green of young pine woods; a late summer sky, pale and transparent. Into this sky a cloud of smoke curled lazily and rose and was dispersed high above a line of birds in flight. The first bird migrations had begun already: from the tundras of Lapland and the Swedish lakes they flew southward in formation, the layers of air vibrating to the movements of their wings; their cries were heard only faintly and occasionally by the small shepherd boy far below, barefoot and carrying a long whip, who raised his head to look; but even when inaudible, they persisted as a presence unseen but felt.

Through the smoke appeared small moving patches of brightness, like mirrors reflecting the sun's rays: scraps of paper, white or discolored, hurled into the air by the heat of the fire. And the wings of pigeons, frightened from their homes, as they circled searching —silver against a dark background—dipping and again soaring up, higher and still higher, finding no place to land.

Lower down the smoke received its tributaries. The bright points that were burning houses in the city were wrapped in the black cottonwool that seeped upward. The slow movement of this viscous mass was broken by the blasts of explosions: spirals of dust rose suddenly here and there, gradually losing speed, dissolving rusty-white plumes in the slow, oily smoke. Red glares appeared suddenly in the balls of smoke, were dispersed, appeared again somewhere else and then finally gave way to blackness.

Below, at the heart of the fire, the great river on which the city stood was a pink metallic ribbon. Ruined bridges lay in it like shipwrecked hulks.

Low down on the horizon, aircraft darted in all directions; and when they disappeared into the smoke there was a volley of explosions. Tanks were firing briskly, quickening their rhythm, hurrying. Mixed with the sounds of artillery fire were the sharp cracks of antiaircraft guns like the uncorking of enormous bottles. At regular intervals, salvos of heavy gunfire thundered with a broader echo and a mortar screeched like the winding of a rusty clock; bombs detonated in quick succession, and then again came the cracks of single shots, and the rising and falling rattle of machine guns.

6

To THE SOUTHWEST the city ended abruptly. There, large modern apartment buildings bordered on fields of oats and potatoes. The streets were marked out but not yet finished, and the few isolated houses in the fields connected only by rough footpaths.

The women who lived there took advantage of any lull in the firing to crawl into the fields and come back with hurriedly dug potatoes and carrots for their children.

That afternoon detachments of the Hermann Goering S.S. Division began to set fire to the buildings.

The plain was a broad quiet panorama. Small groups of people carrying bundles and parcels walked quickly across it, some pushing barrows and handcarts, some carrying long sticks to which were fastened white handkerchiefs. Crickets chirped in the corn, which was red from the glare of the fires. The people kept turning to look back at the blocks of buildings where flames were already flickering in the windows. They wondered whether the fire had yet reached the window they knew so well; which piece of their furniture was burning at that moment. The glare was reflected in the eyes of a cat, clutched feverishly to the bosom of a woman in a printed summer dress. A small boy talked to a canary he carried in a cage. Driven by the single desire to escape, they all walked straight ahead without stopping to think where they were going or why.

To the right of the district that was burning stood rows of unfinished apartment houses of red brick. In front of them an attack was developing. A few tanks rolled slowly forward, churning up the dry soil of the potato fields. Taacoo—taacoo—taacoo—the echo answered their fire. After each shot a spiral of brick dust rose from the buildings, and when it settled, strangely shaped holes broke the symmetry of the windows.

On a whistle-blast from their commander, small figures in gray-green uniforms rose from the ground and ran forward, crouching low. This lasted only a moment, then the whole line of men disappeared again into the dusty green of the potato fields. From the apartments a few single rifle shots answered. Tiny clouds of dust rising along the line of the running soldiers marked where the bullets struck. Again the small figures rose to their feet and again the little puffs of dust appeared; but now they were more numerous. A longer blast on the whistle. The soldiers ran in the opposite direction. The tanks were turning back. The attack was over.

The fields were flooded with a double light—the glare from the burning city and the glare from the setting sun. Flocks of sparrows flew low over the oat fields. The surface of the road leading to the airdrome was iridescent with the colors of the rainbow. A light breeze stirred the dress of a dead woman lying like a discarded doll by the side of the road. Some Russian soldiers of the *Hilfskorps** were moving unsteadily backward and forward, zigzagging wildly, their knees splayed out. In the deserted landscape, against the backdrop of the burning city, they were teaching each other—with much shouting and laughing—how to ride a bicycle.

7

GREAT PYLONS OF reinforced concrete and the network of power cables that they supported followed the track of the suburban streetcar which ran west across the plain. Every few minutes a three-coach

* An auxiliary brigade of Russian ex-prisoners of war under German command.

train passed along the track. On the back platform stood steel-helmeted police, the barrels of their automatic weapons jutting over the guard rail. Tightly squeezed in the grim, terrified crowd, Professor Gil felt someone grip his arm. Round blue eyes looked at him out of the gray face of a workman.

"I know you, professor," the man was saying through tight lips. "We've got to jump now or we'll rot at Auschwitz." The coach tilted on the curves, the pylons flashed by. "There's still time. There'll be no chance later. But it shouldn't be too difficult now. They've got enough people. They're not itching to shoot. You've got to jump forward. If we jump out on different sides we'll have a better chance."

Professor Gil was holding his wife's hand and stroking it gently. Had it not been for the crowd pressing around them, she would not have had the strength to stand up. He saw her head with a scarf tied around it. She did not raise her eyes. He tried by the movement of his fingers to express everything—his love and his pity, the fact that he was with her and that all that had happened since they had been surrounded by the men of the Russian *Hilfskorps* was of no importance.

"No," he said, "I don't care. I shall stay with my wife."

The man turned his head. Shouts and oaths rose from the human mass thrown from side to side by the movement of the train. The man was making his way to the edge of the platform. Several minutes passed. "He didn't jump after all," thought the professor and, at the same moment, he heard yells and the crack of a rifle. The train did not slow down. Voices were raised, each saying something different: "I see him, he's alive"—"No, he's been hit"—"He's all right."

As he fell the man knew that everything now depended on something already past—the force with which he had pushed himself away from the platform. "As long as I don't fall on the rail," he thought and suddenly the rail flashed past his eyes and he felt the impact of the ground on his hands and face. His body knew that it had to get up, but for a moment it lay still, exhausted by the violence of its effort. When he lifted his head he saw the train disappearing in the distance. He rolled to the bottom of the embankment and ran his hands over his face. They were covered with blood. He cleaned them on some grass and then crawled on all fours to the field of stubble. Bent double, he ran towards some potato beds, and when he thought he was far enough from the track to be safe, threw himself into a furrow.

He felt his knees, moved his wrists: no bones were broken. He was free. He turned on his back, trying to distribute the pain he felt at every movement. The evening sky was overcast and smoke from the city mingled with the clouds.

In the middle of the night he awoke. High above droned the engines of airplanes, and leaning on his elbow, he listened. In the darkness that was already tinged with red above Warsaw, brighter red spots were appearing and arranging themselves into long straight lines. These crossed each other or ran parallel; they rose upwards at an angle from many sides, filling the space with the movement of small restless stars. Search-lights probed the skies. "They've got there, have they? But whose are they?" he wondered lazily.

His nostrils were full of the smell of the soil. He was trying to imagine who the men were flying past high overhead in the invisible machines which were the targets for German artillery.

He was alone, one man on the great, dark earth. Everything that had just happened was turning around inside him like a soundless phonograph record: speed was still there but not the sound. Suddenly cut off from all that had gone before, from the city in which he had lived since childhood, he was overcome by a feeling of security. "Let it burn," he said to himself. "What does it matter to me?" A release from duty: he had done what was expected of him and now he need only look on without joining in. That was good. But immediately there came a surge of shame and with it, hatred.

God damn the lot of them. Their bright, warm cafés, their automobiles, the clothes of their women—while he and others like him had to exist from day to day, to earn a miserable wage, to subsist and nothing more. How had he let himself be drawn into it after all, ever since the first year of the occupation? Fighting the Germans for the motherland. The words always rang false; nothing was ever explained clearly. Things won't be the same as they were before the war; another world, happiness for all—but an undefined happiness; and everybody saying: First of all the Germans must be beaten. One couldn't withdraw; one had some pride; and so it went on and on. And it was he who did the work; every night he would cover the bulb with paper, place a revolver within reach of his hand, tie on an apron, and sit over his type. And the street below. He felt cheated—the sentences he had set up, the daily risk of death, the Gestapo who had come to arrest him just when he had gone out to buy bread, changing his name, the doomed city—all these things were somehow merging into one. Over and done with: quite pointless. Never again.

He remembered Gil. That was something different. The editor didn't much like Gil's articles, which were published only occasionally. He called them "intellectual bla."

"You're a dreamer, Martyniak," he used to say, pulling the manuscripts from his bootleg. "A philosopher with a revolver." But Gil didn't lie like the others. One could learn something from him.

The earth. Dogs barking in the distance. Now he was thinking only that he existed, that above him was the sky in which distant engines were humming. He was trying to distinguish the moving lights from the stars.

8

THE AIRCRAFT DROPPING arms and ammunition into Warsaw had to come a long way. They took off from Bari, on the lower edge of the Italian peninsula, flew over the whole southern half of the Continent, and came at last into Poland across the mountain ranges. The Russians had refused them permission to land on their airstrips, and planes which broke through the antiaircraft barrages and completed their missions had to return to base by the same route. Their crews were Polish and British.

Edmund Lompa, a private in the S.S. Hermann Goering Division, found a black notebook in the fields near Warsaw in the wreckage of a crashed airplane. He kept it as a souvenir. He had seen the end of that machine: hit over the city, it rapidly lost height, tugging behind it a long tail of fire. Lompa, a Silesian, spoke Polish with his parents at home. Conscripted into the S.S., he had served on various fronts. After the war he did not know what to do with himself. His parents had remained in Silesia but he was afraid to return there, so he joined the French Foreign Legion and was sent to Indochina. It was only in 1946 that the black notebook reached the hands of the Reverend Nathan Hawkes in Hobart, Tasmania. On the last page, his son had written this:

A detail. On my way to Julia. Thick walls, gray shadow. A dense vine and in it a window. On a rough well-worn wooden table an earthenware jug and bread; a family at supper. Behind them an open door and a bright light shining from behind it. In the half-darkness wine in glasses, ruby against the light. Bare hands on the table; the tangibility, the solidity of a strong human body. Necks. "My girl has a transparent neck, against the light you can see what she's eating and drinking." Behind the people, pans on the wall. The gleam of polished brass. You can only express things properly by details. When you've observed a detail, you must discover the detail of the detail. That Italian family; the very glasses, their hands, each of their faces and the brass pans: an infinity of colors and shapes. Yet a detail ceases to mean anything when it becomes nothing but a color and a shape, when we feel it's a detail and nothing more. People shouldn't paint pictures.

Today I told Julia that I'm going to stay here after the war. Poor Betsy. "An Englishman Italianate is a devil incarnate." To live where there are fewest abstractions, and most details. Human lives are distributed unevenly. For some, the same space is filled with a thousand details; to others—only shades, reflections, the sea, the earth, supper—and that's all. My bay: an abstract notion. I didn't know in the past how to look. One can only learn to see where people have small objects, old customs established for centuries, ancient walls. The war is good in spite of everything.

With Julia, above the village, between olives, near old wine-barrels. What they write in the books we read in school is meaningless to the pupils. They think of it as something "written to sound well." But nothing could ever be real were we not able to experience this happiness.

9

CADET OFFICER SEAL was bending over his bench, concentrating hard. Tight-lipped and with closed eyes he was filing the metal. His grease-covered overalls, which had once been blue, were too large for him and made his long, bent body look bulbous and flabby. On his arm he wore a crumpled Home

Army brassard. Seal owed his nickname in the underground to his sleepy, rolling movements and to the fact that at school he had been champion swimmer of his class. The whole cellar was full of the sounds of drilling and filing and the clanging of hammers. Facing him against the light coming in through the door stood a boy in an S.S. battle jacket with a steel helmet on his head. A hand grenade was stuck in his belt.

Seal raised his head.

"Fifteen. We can't manage more."

The boy swore.

"Can't you make it twenty? We've run out of revolver ammunition."

"You're not the only ones. We can't keep up with it. And I've got to warn you. They won't be the same as the last ones. There's no material left."

"What are you going to make them from?"

"We're cutting up water pipes. Haven't you had any of them yet? Look." He showed him one.

The boy stared at him in disbelief.

"God! Will it work?"

"Yes, of course: it's been tested."

The cellar shook with the broad echoes of explosions.

"How are you off for everything else? Did you get anything from the parachute drops?"

"Two bazookas. Colonel Rog's boys got all the ammunition. We're haggling with them now. The rest's what we captured."

"Have you got bottles?"

"Not those self-igniting ones. We've only got the

ones with celluloid fuses—bits of film. You have to light them."

"How are things? Hot?"

"Not bad today. Two wounded. They sent over a goliath* yesterday. We set it on fire and killed the Huns, but we lost five of our boys."

"What happened to the goliath?"

"It exploded. Damned shame."

"A damned shame. All that TNT."

"See you tomorrow then?"

"Tomorrow."

Seal went back to work. It was the best one could do. Things were bad—very bad. But he felt the quiet anger inside him changing to something else—he was not quite sure what. During the few weeks which had passed since the beginning of the rising he had experienced so many different moods.

It had all started at five o'clock in the afternoon. He was walking along the street to call on Artym, an elderly Socialist leader. The rising couldn't start, of course; it was known that it had been called off. Under the circumstances it would have been insane. He wanted to talk to Artym about what to do next now that the country had two rival governments. Then suddenly he noticed that people in the street had started running. He looked around and saw a column of young fellows advancing along the pavement behind him and noticed that many people were coming out of the houses to join it. At the head of the group

* A small remote-control tank filled with dynamite that exploded on impact.

walked a fat blond man, solemnly carrying an automatic rifle. He kept shouting, "Forward! Forward!" and the others responded uneasily. Seal had a glimpse of their uncertain movements as they pressed close behind their leader; he noticed the barrels of the weapons they were carrying: double-barreled shotguns. The crowd of passers-by who were running suddenly thickened, turned back on itself, and began to disappear into doorways. From the shelters near the German buildings at the street corner came the chatter of machine guns. The group of boys scattered. Following them, Seal reached a staircase and stopped, out of breath. Beside him stood a slim schoolboy. He looked about seventeen. His dark hair fell down over his forehead and he was fumbling nervously in his pockets. He produced in turn a small hand grenade, some crumpled paper, a piece of string, and a dirty comb with broken teeth. Except for the hand grenade, he was unarmed. "Through the courtyard! Get out! Follow me!" shouted the fat blond commander. The boy hesitated. He took a few steps and then stopped. Seal saw that he was trembling. His teeth were chattering and he was moving his tongue over his parched lips. Suddenly he bent forward and ran after the others.

10

THIS NERVOUS BOY was frightened. In his consciousness there were still algebra problems, erotic daydreams, thoughts about rivers, unknown cities, far-off countries. In the warmth of his body at dawn everything he might one day become was wound up tightly like a small spring. Each impact of his foot on the ground carried him on an enormous flight above the world. Freedom, space. There were hundreds, thousands of ancestors in him, uncharted centuries of heredity. Ancestors who hunted wild beasts and drew their shapes on the walls of caves, who raised wheat and drank from earthenware jugs in the heat of harvest time. Ancestors who wrote with a stylus on wax tablets. And the seed of generations to follow him, of unknown people in whom the trace of his smile might be preserved, the way he bent his head, his individual desires or his destiny. Now there was only the wide empty street under machine-gun fire, and his companions. He couldn't let them down. He would have liked to hold on to his mother and cry. He was weak in this pitiless moment, when he had to advance knowing that he—who not so long ago had worn a sailor's suit and sailed small boats on the pond—was now a target for bullets. But he knew too that things could not be otherwise.

Seal, looking at him, felt vaguely ashamed. He knew that a frontal attack on the German shelters stood no chance at all. ("Where did they get the shotguns from?" he wondered angrily.) But by this foreboding of defeat he was only masking his own lack of readiness, his lack of acceptance.

A small, fair woman with a pink child's face filled his mind completely as if he were only a cloak covering her body. He couldn't understand: it was impossible to be separated from Catherine like that—abruptly, in the middle of a conversation he had

47

broken off by slamming the door. The first quarrel of their married life—and they'd only been married a month. Why had he behaved so badly? Run back to her, explain, kiss her feet, beg forgiveness. Many days would pass, each like a year, before his passionate longing to get back to the center of the city, where Catherine was, would ease a little. He had to see her, even for a brief moment, even if he should get killed. He mustn't die first. Astonished at the conflict between desire and reality, he refused to admit defeat. Until one morning he would understand at last that his folly was useless, that he would get no further than the Old City, and that he would have to accept the inevitable as others had done—would have to live as if his previous life had never been.

A public square, dug up during the war for vegetable gardens. It was dusk, he was running, each step brought him nearer to Catherine. The swish of tracer bullets, and he dropped into a bed of potatoes. The tracers curved toward him. He clung to the ground, terrified by the luminous bullets whose course and speed he could watch. He felt them as a dry splitting of the air. An old dream: he had dreamed that he was being pursued by a light which burned everything living on earth. He had fled; it had caught up with him; he had died, and then woke up. In front of him a low wall divided the gardens. "The moment I start to climb over it they'll get me." On the other side of the open space, where there was no wall, two figures appeared suddenly. A boy in military boots, breeches, and a long elegant coat. He strode forward in a slightly theatrical manner, sticking out his hand in which he held a revolver. Behind him came a girl with long hair, wearing a jacket and with a bag slung from her arm. They got across safely. "I've got to do it too. She's waiting," Seal muttered to himself, and soundlessly crying "Forward!" jumped on the wall, conscious that his back was exposed to the deadly menace of fiery whips. He tumbled down on the other side. "So dreams don't always come true," was his first thought.

He was sitting at a round table; his hostess was pouring coffee. Modern pictures, fabrics, pottery, cups with gold rims rattling a little because of the firing. She was smoking a cigarette in a long holder. Her husband, a lawyer, put down an Aldous Huxley novel. "You won't get through that way. There are German positions there. But it will all be over any minute now. Paris has been taken. The Russians are crossing the river. Listen—you can hear their guns." There was shouting under the windows, and shots from a tank. The door flew open, a crowd of young boys in blue overalls and berets appeared, with bottles and grenades in their hands. She tried to stop them: "For God's sake don't start anything! If you do they'll burn the house down." They took no notice of her, rushed to the window, and threw grenades. Explosions; glass was strewn over the fabrics; cups flew off the table and dropped on Seal, the lady, and the lawyer, who were lying flat on the carpet.

He was prying up flagstones with a pickax, thinking with despair that every hour increased the distance between him and Catherine, that perhaps he might get through, that he should try another direction, through other streets. They were building a barricade. When the job was done he had no strength left to think. He lay on a lawn; the August night was deep blue, the courtyard silent, the only sound the crackle of flames consuming a nearby house, their red light reflected on the wall. Suddenly in the darkness, he heard a low sound like somebody clearing his throat—oddly pitched. He heard it again. He got up and crept to the window where the sound seemed to have come from. In the glare he saw a table and on it a quart bottle of vodka, then the heavy face of a stout man, cut in deep lines (a business man? a doctor?) and a thin face with a mustache (an old master-mason? a streetcar conductor?). They lifted their hands and the glasses clinked. "Cheers" they both said and tossed down the liquor noisily. Immobile, silent, they sat and drank in darkness. Seal softly laughed. But suddenly he realized that in that grim, drunken ritual, in those set faces that might have been cut in stone, there was this: they knew, and they had no hope.

11

THE COLONEL WAS brushing plaster dust from the map with his hand. The white powder which had covered everything when a bomb destroyed the part of the block overlooking the courtyard, was settling now. The colonel was blinking his bloodshot eyes, trying to get rid of the flourlike stuff which covered his face. His long nose with violet, sclerotic veins jutted from his whitened face like a clown's. The commander of the group, a short, thickset man, was holding his German helmet on his knees. Unthinkingly he traced a line on its dusty surface. Good manners prevented him from putting it on his head during an air raid. He looked at the colonel without friendliness. He didn't much like these cavalry officers.

"The situation was already quite clear on the day the Germans broke through to the river. Then there was still a choice. Now they've only got four isolated quarters of the city left to liquidate."

"With the exception of the south. So far as we know, we still hold the riverbank there."

"By now it's not certain that we do."

"We've got to hold out. You know the orders. Our government . . ."

The group commander stuck out his lower lip.

"The Russians won't budge."

"It's the only solution left."

"I wanted to break through to Kampinos. We might have saved the youngsters. I can't stand by and watch these children being slaughtered."

"We won't break through now. It's too late. Anyway, we couldn't have escaped. The Germans would have killed off the entire civilian population."

"I've carried out my orders. I've already lost half my effective force. The civilians are doomed, anyway. These old houses are crumbling like rotten trees."

"What's morale like?"

"My men will fight to the last."

The colonel was wiping his face with a handkerchief and, reaching to the back of his neck, was trying to pick pieces of plaster from inside his collar. He asked:

"What about the People's Army? I can't understand them. What do they think? Where are their allies?"

"They've lost nearly all their officers. I'm not sure, but I think some of them plan to pass through the sewers to Zoliborz."

"We've got the entrances to the sewers well guarded."

The group commander was looking at the wall on which darker patches marked the places where pictures had hung once.

"The Old City's the worst quarter to defend—all those damned narrow streets and old houses. Practically nothing left of it now. There's a water shortage. It's only a matter of days."

"And then?"

"We've got to try a breakthrough to the center."

The colonel considered this, slowly nodding his head.

"The possibilities should be investigated. The German positions around the Saxon Garden are strong. It would be a last resort."

"Surprise is the only chance of bringing it off. The civilian population mustn't know or there'll be a panic."

"We should put the plan up to HQ."

The colonel wanted to ask the man sitting opposite what he thought about the possibility of defending

52

the city center and if he were really convinced that no help would come. But he said only:

"Our action is a gesture to the world. The world cannot look on with indifference. Warsaw is writing a page of eternal glory."

The group commander lowered his eyes.

"We must try to find, at all costs," he said, "a means of saving at least some of our men."

12

I SHALL NEVER see Catherine again. Her face has become blurred and I can no longer remember her smile. What is the affection one has for another human being if time can destroy it. And so immeasurable a time: not its length, but the strain of it and its intensity. I'm not twenty-four any more—I'm at least thirty-five.

Was there ever a Catherine? Am I different now from what I was when I first met her? Or perhaps it doesn't matter—as the distance covered by an engine on a side track where it's been shunted for a moment isn't counted? Here, on this spot of earth, everything will be fulfilled for me. Out of all the places, cities, countries, continents—on this little spot only. Sixteenth-century houses, their façades shorn of reliefs and ornaments by exploding steel. Wine vaults, printing houses—from their windows rivers of rubble mixed with pages of vellum books pour like scree down a mountain. Crypts of convents and churches where men and women sing in chorus hymns of intercession and, at the same time, push those who are weak and ailing deeper inside, further from the entrance: to help God, not to be buried alive, to get out of the ruins on all fours, like that woman who carried a child covered with blood, screaming for help, begging people to dig out her other child who had remained inside, not realizing that the child in her arms was dead. The stunned stupor of the survivors: they had prayed, had faith, the priest in the cellar had celebrated Mass and said that their cause was God's cause, that God would not forsake them. They had a feeling of security then, the magic of the words of the old hymn confirming the instinct hidden deep inside themselves which said: it is impossible that that which I am should vanish into nothing. People with whom they held hands a moment ago, shook now in the agony of death; a splinter of metal put an end to all those days, nights, hours—Johnny sit up, Johnny sit up straight, how much is six times seven, I'll buy you a pocketknife if you're good, Johnny's a good boy. Festering stumps, bloated flies buzzing in basements transformed into hospitals, the stench, the animal roars of people being operated on without anesthetic. And incessantly before one's eyes, like a constant throbbing, the rhythm of the world, enormous eruptions of dust, earth, and bricks. The world is an eruption. That is how the planets began; in space everything erupts and explodes through millions and millions of years; what had been on earth lasted no longer than the flight of a moth from light to light. Now all returns to the original condition —the eternal explosion of matter.

The Old City was surrounded. The enemy was attacking from the south and at the same time closing in on the city center from the north to prevent the insurgents in the two quarters from joining forces. In the west, they threw in tanks, goliaths, and infantry against the defenders' positions. In the narrow streets around St. John's Cathedral there was continuous shellfire; a battle raged for every corner of a wall; helmets of German infantry and of insurgents appeared side by side through the white clouds of pulverized masonry; there was sudden amazement, the shock of unexpected encounters, the throwing of hand grenades, bursts from automatic weapons, tongues of fire from the flame throwers which burned men alive, left them writhing, abandoned by their comrades who looked on from a distance wondering how many rounds they had left.

In moments of silence the two sides could hear each other: from the German side an accordion and songs of the Rhine vineyards; from the insurgents' a piano on which a skinny student from the Conservatoire was playing Chopin, with his revolver on the floor underneath his chair. To the north of the Old City was the area of the ghetto that had been destroyed in 1943; a fortnight or even ten days ago it was possible to break through that way to Zoliborz, which was in the hands of the insurgents, and thence to the forests. Now the Germans had brought in an armored train, and from positions in the ruins were attacking the houses guarding the entrance to the Old City. Their Stukas flew low over the roof tops. As the bombs broke away from the fuselage, the faces of the pilots could be seen clearly by people lying flat on the ground who lifted their eyes to see what new destruction was being wrought. The Stukas did not have far to come; they took off from an airstrip on the other side of the city, dropped their loads, and turned back immediately so as not to cross the line of the Vistula. From the windows of houses on the embankment one could see the German gun positions, beyond them the river and the further bank, on which—though no one knew precisely where—the Russians were.

Seal had asked to be transferred to the front line. When he stumbled with the others over bomb craters or crawled along on his belly, he had a feeling of achievement; everything that had happened before seemed clear to him. Now again, for brief moments, he could almost touch Catherine, her fair lashes lowered, her face peaceful and smiling, on the verge of sleep. Now he had to perform his duty; this alone was important. He thought of himself as old, that he had lived his allotted span. He was well armed—an armorer can always pull strings—he carried a Sten gun.

But there was never a definite ending, life was never rounded off, what was to have been a postscript continued to grow, complications arose, new people appeared, and time brought changes.

A high building stood on the edge of the ruined ghetto. From its windows one could see the grayish pink expanse of ruins already overgrown with weeds. Only eighteen months ago houses had stood here, and from their windows Jewish insurgents had fired their revolvers at the Germans. He remembered the weeks of that spring. The weapons he had repaired on the orders of his Socialist group were sent into the ghetto. But apart from this, he had been only a spectator. He had stood in a crowd in Krasinski Square while children ran about looking at the German guns. He saw the movements of the barrels when the guns fired, the windows at which a hand appeared, the falling pieces of masonry. "Oh! They've got him," the crowd shouted. "There—look—he's hanging from the window!" The wind carried the smoke from the burning ghetto toward the churches from which people were issuing, wearing their Sunday clothes, chattering, and moving through the fair grounds where girls' dresses fluttered on merry-go-rounds. Old women were saying anxiously: "They're burning the Jews now. It will be our turn next." Here, in that space, was the memory of a hundred thousand deaths, of two hundred thousand deaths, of five hundred thousand deaths—each different, individual, interrupting a different love, a different desire, a different hope. Now, in the autumn sunshine the wormwood —its roots embedded in greasy ashes, in clots of earth, fertilized by blood—waved in the breeze. Among the bushes German soldiers were deploying light artillery. Far away, behind this desolate region, was the white skyline of the northern boroughs.

The house was solidly built. Shells had torn pieces from the walls, but had not done any major damage so far. From the windows, the defenders had a good field of fire and kept the Germans from getting too close. The neighboring house, several hundred yards away, was already in the hands of the enemy.

In the cellars girls were cooking soup (they had nothing but sacks of beans). There, too, those who had been relieved slept on the floor. Most of them were seventeen- and eighteen-year-old schoolboys: boy scouts of death, with the movements of veterans, in steel helmets which seemed enormous above their thin necks. There were some older men too. Gradually, Seal began to be aware of these people gathered together as individuals, and the tensions that existed among them. As in a submarine during action, nothing could be kept private, except for brief moments when the battle raged with special intensity. Each carried the whole of his past life with him.

13

DAN, THE LEADER. Before the war he had been a regular officer, a second lieutenant in the artillery. His head was wrapped in a bandage, the corners of his mouth were pulled down as if the skin of his face were too tight. He had a supply of vodka which he drank in moderation, keeping himself in a state of semi-intoxication but never getting drunk.

Michael. Before the war he had been known as the theorist of the "national revolution"; under the occupation, publisher and editor of an underground paper in which he advocated a social order based on Catholicism and dictatorship, like the Salazar regime in Portugal. He had a short straight nose and fair reddish hair beginning to thin at the forehead. His head seemed small above his broad square shoulders. He was tall, with long arms and spadelike hands. He had come here after a bomb had smashed up the printing plant from which, during the first weeks of the rising, he had published bulletins for distribution among civilians and soldiers. His wife, a Red Cross nurse, was in the Old City at her hospital. Dan treated Michael with respect and backed him against Bertrand.

Bertrand. It was difficult to find fault with him because he was an exceptionally good shot. Yet in Dan's eyes he had many failings. A twenty-two-year-old student at the Technical College, with a pale, round, calm face and dark eyes, he made no secret of his contempt for the army and for war. His companions in the battalion scornfully called him a pacifist. One day he had brought a wounded German to safety under fire. There was something in him which made people circumspect in his presence. He was not quite "one of us"; his way of thinking was strange and he stressed his aloofness by sudden silences in midsentence and by tolerant smiles. Seal knew that Bertrand had adopted his *nom de guerre* in honor of Bertrand Russell. After the war he wanted to devote himself exclusively to mathematical logic. For Bertrand, Michael's presence was a tragedy. He forced himself to be friendly, but a few words exchanged with Michael were enough to make him walk away discouraged. He suffered, for Michael's presence made him doubt the wisdom of what he had done, deprived his sacrifice of its purity. "This man's a fascist," he said to Seal once, "and I've got to associate with people like him!" Michael was aggressive and made malicious remarks about rationalists and liberals. Dan listened to them with obvious pleasure. He could not forgive Bertrand his passion for abstruse theories and books.

59

The medical orderly Vila was a short, fat girl of eighteen, with white skin and reddish hair. Loud, despotic, she got obedience from the boys by the very strength of her vitality. She interlarded loud prayers with a series of curses based on variations of "arse" and "shit." Completely extroverted, she never tried to conceal her fear and would exclaim: "Holy Mother of God, I'm scared!" But at the same time she never backed out. Her exclamations seemed to have no connection with herself, to apply to somebody else.

The medical orderly Magda was slim with a slightly snub nose and rather colorless blue eyes. One hardly heard her. Seal was present once when Bertrand—for whom she was pouring out some soup—made one of his ponderous remarks. She snapped back at him in precisely the same vein, and it was funny to watch Bertrand's look of amazement while she moved away, as much an automaton as before. But Magda became a real personage after her experience with Captain Osman.

No one knew anything about Captain Osman's past. He wore a uniform like an air force officer's, dyed black. He had a crumpled yellow face, long folds around his wide, capricious, mobile mouth, an ironical expression in his eyes. Over his left eye he wore a black patch, on his head a black beret. Sometimes he would disappear for twelve hours at a time, would be given up for lost, and then reappear and make a short report. He was busy chasing the Germans or—as the men used to say—chasing his own death. He would crawl into the ruins of the ghetto and fire at the enemy gun crews. Often he would sit with his rifle on the steps leading to the turret on top of their house, waiting for some movement in the windows of the house occupied by the Germans. As soon as they began to fire, he would move into the open and shake his fist at them.

The story about Osman and Magda was this. Magda asked Osman to take her with him to the top of the house. He asked her whether she wouldn't be afraid. No. Was she sure she wouldn't be afraid? She was quite sure. They climbed to the top floor and Osman showed Magda a large hole from the floor to the ceiling, made by an artillery shell. "Stand there and show yourself to the Germans," he ordered. She looked at him blankly. "You said you wouldn't be afraid." "But they'll start shooting at me." "Exactly. That's what I want. When they start firing, I'll see them and pick them off." Magda was afraid but she was ashamed to admit it. "I just showed my head," she said later, "and I pulled it back again at once, but the Germans started to fire like mad." Osman called Magda to his window and, taking her hand, pointed her finger at something: against the background of gray blankets screening the window in the enemy house, hands and a blond head were hanging limply. The hands moved, the Germans were pulling the dead man back by his legs. Thus did the line of Magda's life cross the lifeline of an unknown man—a watchmaker from Heidelberg, a workman from Berlin, or a farmer from the Black Forest—nobody would ever know who he was.

14

THE CONFLICT BETWEEN Dan, Michael, and
Bertrand reached its pitch the day Father Ignatius
appeared. He was sitting on a bench in what used to
be the washroom, drinking water from a bottle, his
Adam's apple rhythmically moving in his taut neck.
From beneath his battle jacket his cassock hung in
tatters like a dirty worn-out skirt. Strapped to his breast
was a tin in which he carried the Host. The news of
his arrival spread all over the house; everybody knew
him—the Jesuit hero. The fact that he had joined them
changed everything; the lonely tension—the tension of
a submarine crew—was eased; for a while the world
regained its order. This was just ordinary war, the
front line; they hadn't been forgotten, a chaplain was
coming around. Seal recognized Father Ignatius; he
knew his real name. He remembered that thin, dark
face with its black eyes and narrow lips—true, he remembered them expressing triumph, sublime satisfaction at mathematical perfection, when Father Ignatius
had turned away from the blackboard covered with
formulas and looked at his audience. Father Ignatius's
lips were blue now, his weary gray face covered with
soot; there was plaster on his nose and cheeks. The
boys approached him, took off their helmets, and knelt
down waiting for the moment when he would hear
their confessions. Bertrand stood apart, looking at him
with his head on one side, his eyes immobile and
greedy, as if he wanted to preserve this picture forever

in his memory. Then he suddenly volunteered to relieve the men on the top floor so that they could make their confessions. Seal saw him hurry upstairs, carrying his rifle in his limp, dangling hand, his head still tilted to one side. Seal felt sorry. He did not think of what he himself would do. To behave differently from the others seemed impossible, unjustifiable. Father Ignatius produced a crumpled purple stole from his pocket. Bertrand's solitary departure contained a painful challenge. No. He couldn't leave Bertrand alone now.

He ran and caught up with him on the stairs leading to the upper floors. Rubble grated under his boots, and Bertrand looked round. The determined expression suddenly slipped from his face and gave way to incredulity and astonishment. He stopped. He smiled softly and gently and his lips trembled as though he had been crying.

They lay side by side on the floor, observing through the holes in the wall the German positions in the ruins of the ghetto. The noise of the battle vibrated in uneven waves through the walls, growing louder and then dying away. Bertrand leaned his head towards Seal, propping it on the hand which was tightly gripping the breech of his rifle.

"Do you know who that is?"

"Yes. I used to meet him during the occupation."

"You know what he uses mathematical logic for?"

"Yes. I do."

Father Ignatius had written a treatise designed to prove by mathematical logic that God existed. During the occupation he had invited a lot of young people to secret lectures held in the Jesuit convent. Seal had heard three. The first two were interesting, though Seal, listening to Father Ignatius and hearing his formulas, had experienced that inner protest you feel when you are forced to follow another person's reasoning, unable to pinpoint the flaws in it yet realizing that there was a flaw somewhere. Of the third lecture he had unpleasant memories. In it Father Ignatius tried to explain the apparent political implications of his metaphysics.

"Seal, have you ever read Thomas Mann's *Magic Mountain?*"

"Yes, I have."

"Do you remember the discussions between Naphta the Jesuit, and Settembrini? I shall be on Settembrini's side to the end."

Yes, Bertrand was right. Father Ignatius was Naphta. "It's odd. I can't recall his face during the third lecture. Why?" Seal could remember only the invectives Father Ignatius hurled at capitalists, Socialists, Freemasons, Communists, democrats; his own embarrassment and disgust that Ignatius was behaving in an undignified way. His only omission had been the Jews who, two kilometers from the spot where the lecture was being held, were being loaded into trucks and driven to gas chambers. Having unfolded the vision of a pure, orderly, ideal society, Father Ignatius called for a crusade: "Don't be afraid to use the most radical measures! Don't be frightened of blood!" After that lecture Seal lost the interest in Catholicism which had been stirring in him, and he held Father Ignatius responsible for the fading of his desire to reread St. Augustine.

But why shouldn't he make his confession? What had that got to do with Father Ignatius? Wasn't it the same as confessing one's sins in front of mountains, or the sky, or the sea? And why should he make it anyway? Whether he did or not was without importance; everything he was and everything the world was could be summed up in the words "to be" and "not to be." He had moments when he felt separated from himself—he saw himself holding his rifle and lying at the bottom of a great precipice; he saw the battle, the city, Catherine (what was Catherine doing now?); he saw the Earth. It was better to be here with Bertrand. Bertrand existed beside him, concrete, alive, needing his help. Seal knew that this moment was important, that it marked the beginning of real friendship. He envied Bertrand his powers of concentration, his stubbornness, his resolution. Bertrand, just as he took the trouble to shave carefully every day and to keep neat and clean in this doomed house, remained loyal to his intellectual attachments. He took mathematical formulas and marksmanship equally seriously and concentrated on each according to circumstances. While Seal was thinking about all this, Bertrand said, watching carefully—too carefully—the perimeter before them:

"The things one reads about come true sometimes. Today's the day of Jesuits like Naphta. Red or black. That's why I shouldn't be alive."

Father Ignatius sat in the courtyard on a flight of steps leading to the cellar. After hearing confessions, he felt within himself the galloping rhythm of other people's lives, other people's affairs and self-denials. These

65

children. He was guilty; he was responsible for their deaths. All through the occupation he had encouraged them to make this sacrifice. He was humanly responsible without any doubt. But was this the proper standard to judge by? At the same time fear paralyzed his legs. To get up again and walk into that hell of exploding shells seemed impossible. He took out a dirty handkerchief and wiped the sweat of fear from his forehead. Slim, frail, black, beside the big, bulky Michael, who was rubbing his shoulders against the steps and leaning backwards on his elbows, he was absorbed in his inner conflict. He kept his eyes closed to prevent Michael from guessing what he was going through. He listened to the sound of gunfire, hoping absurdly that it would cease suddenly, that everything would be over before he had to get up. He asked Michael:

"Have they all made their confessions?"

"All except two upstairs. They don't want to."

"Communists?"

"No, but of the same crowd. Students. One's a rationalist; his head's stuffed with all this logical positivist rubbish. I've seen the second on and off for a long time. Comes from a Socialist family, I believe. Suffers from inbred radicalism."

The priest was fighting the fear which he felt in his body as a repulsive disease—a disease strictly individual, exclusively his own, that couldn't infect anyone else.

"Michael, where can a human being draw his strength from if he rejects the only source of strength? These young people whose confessions I heard. What

66

are their sins? One asked me if it was a sin to have fired at a German though he knew he was wounded. These youngsters are strong with the strength of their own purity."

Michael stroked his stubble-covered chin.

"For many—for these boys—fighting's only a duty. A duty towards God and the motherland. But for some it's a form of suicide."

The priest turned his face towards the sun, the calm sun of defeat, a burning circle which rolled behind the clouds of smoke.

"So many deaths. All our hopes, the flower of the nation. You've got to be blind not to see where it all comes from. Their civilization! The Renaissance, the Age of Enlightenment, rationalism, democratic catchwords. The alliance of American plutocrats and Bolsheviks. The West. The West. That West will understand one day what has happened here, but it will be too late by then!"

Michael snorted.

"It's more convenient for them this way. They've saved the lives of their own soldiers. Lives, above all. But the quality of the lives doesn't matter."

"The Church was right when it fought usury. Their rationalists, their crazy reformers: they only try to find arguments to justify filling their own pockets. Once they've filled them, they don't want to die."

Father Ignatius got up suddenly. Towering over Michael, he violently thrust out his chin—the chin of a Warsaw Savonarola.

"They'll cling frantically to life. They'll call in barbarians from the steppes to help. And the barbarians know the price of their blood. They must be repaid in towns, countries, the extermination of the innocent. But the Roman Empire of cowards will fall."

After Father Ignatius's departure, Michael gave up any further attempt to discuss things with Bertrand. From then on he was silently polite to him and Seal. Dan looked at them askance. Both showed their disapproval in their attitude. The spiritual bond—the bond which should unite the crew of any ship that sails on seas of destruction—was broken.

15

No one witnessed Captain Osman's death. During Father Ignatius's visit he had been away on one of his expeditions, and after his return, he spent a lot of time in the turret as usual. A fresh detachment going into action was just crossing the courtyard when Captain Osman's black beret fell at their feet. They rushed upstairs. He lay on his back, his face streaked with blood as if it had been tattooed, his arms spread wide. They stood over him, some of them blowing their noses to keep back their tears. To these boys Osman was the object of silent hero-worship; their imagination was stirred by the unknown motives of his lonely courage. Dan bent down and searched the pockets of Osman's black uniform. He pulled some papers from his wallet, and read aloud his real name. Some photographs of a young woman fell out: her head with its smoothly combed hair was inclined towards the little girl she held on her lap. Dan shut the wallet and buttoned it into the pocket of his jacket. "So he had a family. We'll have to find them and hand over his things." They carried him carefully downstairs and buried him in the courtyard beside the others, strewing earth mixed with brick dust on the black uniform. They put the black beret on his forehead to cover the wound made by a percussion bullet.

That night Seal was holding Magda's hand, not thinking about anything, hardly breathing at all—so that thought and breathing should not frighten away her presence. The house was dark; before them was the ghetto in which, in the light of sudden flashes, the wormwood bushes seemed thickened and enlarged, as in a quiet garden during a summer storm.

It was in this changing light that they noticed a group of white figures standing motionless. Seal thought he was seeing things. So did the others. Were they the ghosts of people who had been murdered there? They kept their eyes fixed on the apparition. Seal realized with shame that he had goose flesh, but it was beyond belief. The figures began to move along slowly. Were they Germans?

"Don't fire!" somebody shouted. And the tone of the voice, which indicated that its owner was watching and had understood, broke the tension. After a moment the voice went on calmly: "They're patients from St. John's Asylum. It was hit."

Now Seal saw them distinctly. In long white sheets, wearing coronets of weeds on their heads, waving green branches, they were celebrating their incomprehensible rites, shaking rhythmically, disappearing in the darkness, then visible again in the red or bluish reflections from the throbbing skies. They walked around each other, turned, and walked back again, the breeze carrying the sound of their monotonous chant.

Vila and Magda had come up from the cellars. At that moment a burst of tracer bullets streamed from the enemy positions towards the white figures. Some fell in a repulsive theatrical flurry of white robes, but the chanting of the rest went on. They danced, jumping on the piles of debris like the gesticulating chorus of an insane tragedy. Magda grasped Seal's hand. He felt the warmth of her palm, then only amazement. The discovery of another human being. A heart pumping warm blood, legs, hands, a small bush of pubic hair, thoughts, the past, the same fear, the same loneliness. He had ceased to be a separate being, everything that made him different was gone. Pity, affection—just because he knew nothing about Magda and need not know anything. And complete security, nothing of what had been, nothing of what would be, the duration of an eternal moment.

The figures disappeared, the space was empty again. Seal remembered orchards seen long ago in the light of distant flashes of lightning. Magda's arm touched his, fear left her hand, which was now in his hand, not understanding. The certainty that in her, next to him, there was not a thought, not a single reaction which would not be identical with that which existed in him. Seconds, minutes, or hours. They were silent, participants and witnesses of a discovery of which there had been no warning.

When she left, he dreamed of the touch of a smooth,

broad river, of its feather-like flow brushing his skin. A little girl with an ugly, boyish face, weeping desperately, holding up her dress, trying to reach a small boat which was being carried away from her. He himself swimming after the boat, wading toward the little girl, the boat between them, a smile on her face besmirched by tears, and he not breathing; a boundless tenderness engulfing him; her thin shoulder blades over which hung a quaint braid of hair; willows and sunshine. Osman with his arms spread wide, his face tattooed with blood, swimming on his back—from unknown cities and countries into unknown countries. He had to pinch his arm for he was dozing off; for the first time in many days he was entering sleep by way of vivid daydreams.

In the sky searchlight beams crossed and recrossed.

"Today the Germans occupied two houses behind us," said Bertrand. "We're almost cut off. Get ready for the fun."

16

THAT NIGHT, ON his way down to the cellars, he felt a light touch on his shoulder. He stopped in the darkness, his heart thumping. The girl took him by the hand. The dusk was soft; rainbow-colored rings flickered before his eyes; he abandoned himself to the guiding hand. He stumbled and a hollow echo sounded from the low ceilings. There was nothing unexpected about her mouth. A return to his own early childhood; the separation of self into two mouths, his mother's and his, or only his, which was the same thing. Her hair was cut short at the back, this he knew, but neither her shape nor the way she moved nor her odor penetrated clearly to his consciousness. Slowly, simultaneously, they were leaning towards the floor and at the same time groping with one hand over the cold tiles, until they found a place where some empty sacks were spread. Again he felt amazed that she was a living, walking, working person, that she had a separate entity, her own, unknown, when in fact she was at one with him from the outset, at the bottom of a smooth precipice that divided them from the world. This had no beginning and no end, there was nothing to fear, there was no death, there was never a barrier between one human being and another; happy islands, naked brown-skinned people, bright flowers, songs of joy, one undivided rhythm. With his cheek close to hers, he heard her inner cry, the cry of triumph.

Then in the darkness her quiet voice.

"This, the sun, and the taste of apples will be the same when we're gone."

His fingers traced out her eyes. The lids were closed and the corners were damp with tears.

Again her low voice, speaking not to him but into space.

"To have time to spare. Old women sitting in front of their houses at dusk."

Under his hand he felt the smoothness of her chin, the shape of her mouth as if carved in stone. Impenetrable darkness, the chill of the floor at his back. Rats scrambled past, squealing, chasing each other along the walls. Catherine's eyelashes. But these two women were strangely identical, one merged into the other, they were fused together, impossible to separate.

She spoke again:

"Perhaps it doesn't matter. One wants to understand, one thinks that by living one will understand the world. In an hour, or by tomorrow, or in a year. And yet one will never understand anything. Perhaps it doesn't matter."

Sarcophagi on which a man and a woman lie side by side on their backs, looking with stony eyes into the darkness through the centuries. The lines of their knees, their elbows touching each other; and high above them, the moon waxing and waning for the thousandth, the ten-thousandth time.

He felt her smiling.

"You're with Bertrand. Good."

He said:

"That you exist. I can't understand it."

Her hand on his cheek. A gentle, indulgent caress. She turned her mouth toward him.

"That boy's suffering too much. You've been through the difficult part already. I think I have too, probably."

And suddenly this desire: to enfold her whole life. Every thing, each of her mornings, days, evenings, the street where she lived, the dresses she wore; to give himself to her completely, all that he was, all he was striving for. It was so difficult.

"Catherine's still somewhere in the city center. She's my wife. I was in despair."

Sarcophagi, and an understanding hand, a hand like

that of his mother who had long been dead. Were there blue veins under the skin, knuckles that stood out, was it narrow? He had not yet seen it.

"Who wasn't? You shouldn't have been."

And then after a while:

"Years, or one fleeting moment. In a fleeting moment to have a home, trees, gardens, children; to live through years. Lots of other people have had to live like that."

He asked:

"Why did you want to go with Osman that day?"

"Because"—she was searching for words—"all human beings are the same. If somebody's capable of doing something, you want to find out why."

He pulled her face towards his:

"My fleeting moment."

"You are for me what I am for you."

The rumble of a distant explosion echoed somewhere upstairs. A door slammed, some masonry fell, and then again there was only the darkness and the silence. An enormous wave was rolling, engulfing the chill and the sun; the familiar shape of her lips against his closed mouth.

"You ought to know who I am. My real name is Joanna. I was born Joanna Gil."

17

LIGHT FROM THE oil lamp shone on the papers. A moth which had got through the closed shutters fluttered here and there and the movement of its wings made the flame flicker. The breech of the sub-machine gun on the edge of the table was striped with moving shadows. Winter, leaning back in his chair with hands folded across his stomach, was listening to the man sitting opposite. A monotonous semitone, a hum which rose and fell. The man's face was sun-burned, worn by years of poverty, undernourishment, and humiliation; his neck, a dirty mass of wrinkles, hung over his coarse linen shirt—which was fastened at his throat by a white button sewed on with black thread. Meek, respectful eyes stared at Winter's mouth, watching for a sign of approval or displeasure.

"Stasiak's the worst of the lot. He walks about frightening people and stirring up trouble. He never says anything straight out—that's the sort of creature he is—just drops a hint here, a hint there, laughs and spits as if he knew better all the time. And people get worried, for he never says straight out that things will be bad—and they just take it for granted that they're going to be. He is the worst we've got in the whole village."

Winter asked:

"How much land has he got? He must be well off himself if he keeps in with the rich."

The man looked scornful.

"Nothing to speak of. Twelve acres—mostly sand. Worthless soil. He used to have a horse that he worked in the state forests. Or he did some ploughing for Jonievicz, the miller, or cut the corn for him. Six kids. A stupid man."

"What does he say?"

The man's eyes moved away from Winter's mouth

75

to the papers, to the submachine gun; uneasy, uncertain.

"Those rich people say: don't take the land, for the masters will come back and the Americans will come. And anybody who's taken land is going to be tried and strung up. But Stasiak doesn't talk like that. He's shrewder. He says the masters aren't coming back. But don't be too pleased, he says; they'll give us land all right but they're out to cheat the peasants and later on they'll herd them into their . . . collectives, as they call them. He says the peasants have always been oppressed and always will be oppressed. If you're clever you'll get out—to the factories, to the towns. The reform is eyewash. That's what he says. The people don't believe the masters are coming back. But they swallow his stories all right."

"And under the occupation? Did he keep in touch with the partisans?"

"Can't say he did, can't say he didn't. His children are small, the oldest boy's twelve. Everybody was frightened of the partisans. Nobody ever said anything against them, as they found out about it at once. And he was always suspicious. He even said privately that no good would ever come from the men in the forest. But never out loud. When the Russians arrested the Jonieviczes, he said nothing out loud except that the gold they'd collected during the war wouldn't help them, nor the vodka they'd given the partisans either."

Winter knew that the soldiers had orders to bring Stasiak in. The information tallied on the whole. The man sitting in front of him probably had no personal score to settle with Stasiak. He was acquiring, for the first time in his life, a feeling of his own importance. A poor insect trodden on by everybody, he was extricating himself at last from the dust of the road. And he knew how to use his head. He'll join the Party; his thick fingers will move slowly along the rows of letters, stopping at the unknown, difficult words. Until, at last, he becomes the most important man in the village. One day he'll be the chairman of the collective farm. His children will go to school and the university, and at the family table names of scholars and famous writers of the past will be mentioned, names they had never heard before.

"One more thing," Winter stopped and looked at the moth which, having burned its wings, was fluttering helplessly on the papers. "When the Gestapo took away the Jews, how did he behave? Did he take any of the Jews' possessions?"

The man took a quick look at Winter's face. (Interesting to see what he'll say. Clearly he doesn't like Jews. He sees that I'm one. Here their solidarity against the Jews is aroused. But if he wants to ruin the other man, this is a good chance.)

"Some did. They divided up the feather beds and furniture. He didn't. I'm not one to say what's not true. Later the wife of that innkeeper, Abraham, escaped from the ghetto and got back here. The headman called together all the village elders and they talked and talked and decided nothing. They were frightened of the Germans and nobody wanted to take it on himself. The Germans came and shot the Jewess in the wood behind the village. Stasiak, who'd always quarreled with the headman, anyway, said the headman sent his boy to the Germans on the quiet and told them. But nobody knows for certain."

"And who's the headman?"

"Bulanda."

Winter took a pencil from the table and wrote down the name.

"But now this Stasiak does us a lot of harm. Yes, a lot of harm."

Winter got up.

"Thank you, citizen. Today power belongs to the people and it will continue to belong to them. To such people as you. And we shall conquer ignorance. Whether they want it or not, the land reform's going through."

Bent over his papers, Winter was thinking about the day that was just past. A difficult day. Those who could help lie low and come stealthily at night. They're frightened. The forests are full of partisans. In the next village two agitators were shot through the window while at their supper. Nobody can find the culprits. Roundups, blood, and more blood; wives lamenting husbands killed by partisans; mothers lamenting sons arrested or killed by us. That vision. A clean structure reaching to the sky, always in the future. His father nodding his head and daydreaming: "My son, this world will go under. It's an evil world, an unworthy world. We are being persecuted and wronged —by people like ourselves who are equally wronged." His father and mother in the ashes of the ghetto on the other side of the Vistula. What was he doing here?

Wasn't he in fact a stranger here, in this country, now that the streets in which he had spent his childhood and the people of whose destiny he had thought when reading Lenin were all gone? Weariness.

The soldier at the door sprang to attention:

"We've brought the man Stasiak, sir."

"Bring him in."

He was a small man with a drooping dark mustache. He blinked as his eyes accustomed themselves to the light. Winter sent the soldiers away and moved up a chair for him; Stasiak sat on its edge, looking at the cap he had placed on his knees. The same kind of neck as the other man who had sat here a short while ago: lattices of wrinkles, uncut hair with blades of straw in it falling over the nape of his neck.

From behind the circle of light Winter said sharply:

"You are agitating in your village against the land reform."

Stasiak slouched. A slurred murmur from beneath his mustache.

"Don't deny it. We know everything. You're trying to oppose the will of the people by whose authority we give the land to the peasants."

The man replied clearly now:

"It is not true. I don't do what you say. The peasants should have the land."

"You're going about telling people that collective farms are going to be set up here. There will never be any collective farms in Poland. The land is being given to the peasants as their property. Do you know what we call a man who spreads false information about the

People's Government? We call him a saboteur. The penalty for that is five years' imprisonment."

Stasiak said nothing. His fingers were loosening and tightening their grip on his cap.

(Why the hell doesn't he say: "I thought collective farms were good things?" He could answer like that. But he's not tricky.)

"In whose interest is it that the peasants shouldn't take the landlords' estates? The interest of the masters who lived by your sweat and your toil. The interest of rich people like Jonievicz, because when the peasants haven't enough land they're compelled to work for them. And you want to help people like that. The People's Government is lifting you up from misery—from neglect. But you don't seem to care at all about your children's happiness. No, you'd rather frighten others so that everything can remain as it was before. So that your children will be as ignorant and poor as you are."

Gray eyes with red veins. Naïve eyes—thought Winter.

"Not at all. It's not so. I never said they shouldn't take the land."

Winter asked unexpectedly (let's see his reaction):

"Do you know Bulanda, the headman?"

"Certainly I know him."

"During the war he was on good terms with the Germans. Yes or no?"

The man's head was motionless. There was a hardly noticeable blush under the brown skin of his cheeks. He stroked his mustache.

"I don't know about that."

80

"And what about the Jewess killed by the Germans? Who betrayed her? Was it Bulanda?"

(How deep-seated are these village feuds? A hidden resentment sets in, stays like a splinter deep in the body—a threat repeated in one's thoughts: "You wait, your time's coming, I'll get you one day." And then the much desired and long awaited moment comes. He has before him an officer who is everything here: authority, the police, the judge. And the officer's a Jew. Now he's afraid. Soldiers have come at night, have dragged him from his bed while his wife and children screamed around him. If he says a word, he'll ruin his enemy, help himself, establish a feeling of confidence between himself and his inquisitor.) Winter propped his chin on his palm and began to twirl a pencil in his fingers. He looked at Stasiak and a furtive smile lifted the corners of his narrow lips. Stasiak did not look at him now. With an effort, as if searching his memory, he said:

"The Germans came, the Jewess was in her house. Either they wanted to see of their own accord that no Jews had been left or somebody had dropped a hint. People are bound to say that someone or other did it, but whoever did won't admit it, and they'll accuse him falsely. People are what they are. They'll always tell tales against each other. Out of spite."

(What am I to do with him? This moral code. Or perhaps only solidarity? He's badly prepared for the times ahead. He won't last. But after all, why should I destroy this poor creature? What good will it do? Terror? Only unrest, whispers, commiseration, one point in favor of the partisans!)

"I could send you to prison now, in the middle of the night. For the harm you have done. How many children have you?"

"Six." Stasiak's cap was screwed into a ball between his fingers.

Winter turned his head sharply toward him across the table. (When I look at people like this, my face is frightening enough by itself.)

"I could send you to prison. But this time I shall forgive you. But remember: if you go on chattering you'll be arrested. We aren't like your former masters or like the Germans. The People's Government knows everything that goes on in the village. Do you understand?"

Stasiak seemed to choke. He was slowly leaning backwards, looking at the officer (always humble, always degraded, always trembling, always hating, thought Winter).

"Yes, sir."

Winter got up and extended his hand to him.

"One day you'll see for yourself what we want. We want your welfare. Take the land and don't prevent others from taking it. This land is yours. No one will ever take it away from you."

18

THERE WAS A long-drawn-out crack like the tearing of heavy silk fabric. The wall caved in and covered the stairs with debris. A shell had come through the window and exploded inside. At the same moment Dan shouted: "Everybody outside—quick!

You with the stretchers, get the wounded out! Michael! Where's Michael?" The dirty bandage on his head came undone and fell over his eyes. He tugged at it violently and tore it off, uncovering a scar right across his forehead that was still bleeding. He stopped, produced a flask from his pocket, drank, and then wiped his mouth on his sleeve. "Michael, man the ground floor on the side facing the German house. The attack's going to come from there. Hold on whatever happens. We'll deal with anyone coming from above or across the field."

A long echo answered the artillery fire. Joanna, Vila, and a few boys with stretchers rushed upstairs. The early morning was cool, the sky a pearly pink. They went into the courtyard. More crashes, collapse of walls, a taste of brick dust spoiling the early morning freshness. Michael grouped around him Seal, Bertrand, and ten others. Bertrand came up to Dan.

"I want to suggest something."

Dan swore, fingering his scar.

"What is it?"

"It would be better not to occupy the upper floors; just concentrate everybody on the ground floor—on the ghetto side and their side. The upper floors can't be held. If they want to finish us off, they'll just send a plane over."

Dan gave him an angry look.

"Nonsense. You can't do anything from downstairs. Besides—I'm going upstairs, not you," he added disdainfully.

And he spat out after Bertrand, who had turned to go:

"Defeatist."

Bertrand turned back, his head on one side:

"Why do you say that when you know it's not true?"

Dan went purple in the face. He shouted:

"I know you all right! You despise everybody here. Pray to Saint Marx that I won't get you some day. You noble, bleeding martyr, you. You think you're the only one who doesn't want to rot."

Michael intervened:

"Let him alone, Dan. What do you want him to do? There's no time for this sort of thing."

The house held by the Germans was silent; no sign of life; the first bright ray of sunlight on its surface; the recesses filled with bluish shadows. It was the hour of hare tracks in the dew, of creaking pump handles at village wells, of an echoing hammer straightening a plough; of geese cackling near a stream, their white wings lifted in the mist. Again an explosion, masonry falling in front of the windows.

Seal whispered to Bertrand:

"You're wasting your time arguing with Dan."

Bertrand put his hands behind his neck:

"I understand him."

Five minutes, ten minutes.

"Stephen," Joanna called Seal by his Christian name. "Come here a moment and help with the wounded."

"Is it all right if I go?" he asked Michael.

"Yes, but come back quickly."

Johnny, the youngest of the garrison, lay on a blood-soaked stretcher. His flaxen hair was hanging in tangles. Paper-thin skin with blue veins.

"I wanted to say goodbye," said Joanna. "We've got to get him out of here at once. He's got to be operated on. He'll die here."

Standing face to face, they clasped both hands. Joanna's were sticky with the blood of the wounded boy.

"Take care of yourself," Seal said inanely.

She smiled, said suddenly:

"Don't slouch," and let her hands fall.

"Hail Mary, full of grace," Vila mumbled, crossing herself, "The Lord be with thee. The two hundred yards to the corner of the street are the worst. Afterward it's plain sailing. Blessed art thou among women and blessed is the fruit of thy womb, Jesus. If only my legs were thinner. Give me some rope. If we don't tie him to the stretcher we'll lose him."

Seal stood in the gateway, leaning against the wall. He felt ashamed to be staying there in safety, and at the same time a part of him realized that to do nothing was an immense relief.

The girls ran from the gateway. Joanna first, bending forward, the burden was almost too heavy for her, and the stretcher rocked. Behind it went Vila's strong white calves and broad backside. They jumped to avoid bomb craters. Near them bits of dirt and paving stones flew up. They ran on and machine guns begin to bark.

Seal dug his fingers into the wall. Suddenly he felt a violent shock as if a spring had been released under him. Uncomprehending, he found himself in the open and felt a blast of air. His legs were torn from under him, and at the same instant he saw Joanna falling forward, the overturned stretcher, Vila on all fours dragging it to one side. The picture came closer, he was taking Joanna in his arms, blood—hers or Johnny's. He was running—oh God, don't let me stumble; great God, don't let it happen, don't let it be that. The gateway; he put Joanna down, tugged at her blouse, and fell on top of her, hurled there by the blast of an explosion. The noise deafened him: He saw the wall of the house tottering and falling and at the same instant realized that Joanna was dead. A crash and darkness. A rush of air as a bomb fell into the courtyard and he felt something hit him in the back. "The others!" Shots in the darkness. "Am I alive?" To be with them. Michael's voice: "Don't let them get any closer. Use your hand grenades." The bright squares of the windows, the ground floor still intact. He recognized Bertrand. Germans were coming out of the sun. "Get that one, that one there!" He fired a burst and a German slid to the ground, screaming. Plaster falling, Michael calling: "Watch your flanks . . ." and a black object hurtled through the window. Seal flung himself head first into the soft layer of rubble on the floor. An explosion; Bertrand dragging a body; the movement of hands throwing grenades. Seal threw his as far toward the flank as he could— the Germans were coming from that direction. "Back," Michael shouted, "they're coming from the field now." It was clear that the upper story was finished, and everybody in it.

Bertrand was dragging a wounded man. Seal jumped

up two steps to help him, and at that moment Bertrand let go and sat down, a look of amazement in his eyes. It lasted only for a second; his face turned white. When Seal stretched his hand to him, Bertrand said "Mother," and fell back, his features stiffening. "Should I carry him? No, not him." Seal took the wounded man under the arms. "His whole back's ripped open." A mass of blood and dust, limp boots bumping on the stairs. It was Gdula, the one who used to imitate Hitler with a piece of broken black comb between his upper lip and his nose.

He heard somebody shouting, "Quick!" The Germans would be here any moment. He turned Gdula over on his stomach and overtook the others. In the gateway was Joanna's body, a shape covered with dust; he stooped, wiped clean the lower part of her face and the half-open mouth in which her teeth gleamed faintly. But they were running now. It was daytime, morning, a bright world, to live, to live. Not yet.

Here was the corner. He jumped into a bomb crater. And suddenly, staring at the damp earth in front of him, he realized what had happened. No one would ever find out, no one would ever know. He felt as if he had killed Joanna himself. He could never tell anybody that Gdula was still alive when he left him. He was shaken by an attack of hysterical weeping. "Hit him on the head," said somebody behind him. "That'll keep him quiet."

19

THE BELL RANG at the gate. Martyniak, still limping after his leap from the train, came out from behind the rows of tomatoes and looked questioningly at his sister-in-law. The vegetable garden was calm in the afternoon sun.

The woman put down her hoe and wiped her hands on her apron.

"I'll peek through the gap in the fence here. If I make a sign, get through the hedge and across the ditch."

She went toward the fence. He followed her with his eyes, ready to run. Having looked through the gap, she turned round and made a reassuring gesture. Then she went back to the gate and began a conversation through the bars. At last she turned the key in the lock.

A stout man with a red face was walking with her toward the house. From a distance, Martyniak recognized his editor. Just as usual, high officers' boots and curly hair. Under his arm he carried a black briefcase. He waved his hand at Martyniak and called out:

"Hello. Haven't seen you for ages. I had a hell of a job finding you."

They shook hands. Martyniak's smile was broad, covering his uneasiness. (So Borkowski's about, is he? What does he want me for?)

"I thought it was the Germans. I didn't know you were alive, Mr. Borkowski."

The other man laughed:

"Oh, I can arrange things, I can manage. I've been caught in a roundup already; something like that happens here every day. But on this line you meet all Warsaw. You've found a nice spot. What a garden," he let his eye wander over the expanse of it. "Plenty of room to hide if anything happens. When did you leave Warsaw?"

"On the fifteenth of August. I jumped from a train."

"Well, that's two weeks ago. And the house with the printing press?"

"Burned down."

Borkowski produced a large handkerchief.

"It's still hot, though the summer's over. I'd like to talk to you, Martyniak. Matters of importance. Privately, if I may."

The gardener's house was built of wood, and one story high, like most of the houses on the outskirts of the city along the railway running west. Martyniak opened a rickety door and led the editor into a room where there was a metal bed, a basin, and a water jug. Seeds were spread out on pieces of cloth on the floor. They sat facing each other, the visitor on the bed, which creaked under his weight, Martyniak on a chair he had pulled up.

"Cigarette? They're pretty foul, not real tobacco."

Stroking his knee with his palm, Borkowski said:

"So we're alive. Polutek's here. I don't know about the others. Probably dead."

Martyniak asked him:

"But Warsaw, Mr. Borkowski? What's going to happen? They'll smash the city to bits."

Borkowski's eyes were absent.

"Nothing can be done. There'll be sacrifices, of course. But the Russians, even if they don't want to help, can't stand still. Strategy will necessarily push them forward. A city's just a city. We shall rebuild it."

He leaned towards Martyniak.

"But now—business. We can't just sit idle, we have to do something. So we're going to start a paper again. We've got the money."

Martyniak was thinking: So this is it. They can never let well enough alone. The city's burning down, and all they want is a paper. And it doesn't really matter to them what sort of paper it is and what's going to be printed in it.

Cautiously he began to sound the other man out:

"Perhaps it's a good idea. But what can we do about it now? We've no paper, no press. And raids every day. How can we organize distribution?"

Borkowski cut him short:

"Don't worry about that. You can buy anything these days. There's plenty of paper. We could even duplicate it. But there'll be a press all right. The Germans will find it for us themselves somewhere in Warsaw. Now they'd deliver Hitler himself provided they're well paid. And the place for it? Here. In the garden shed. It couldn't be better."

Martyniak considered how best to begin. At last he said:

"You've said yourself, Mr. Borkowski, that the Russians are coming."

The other man struck his knee with his fist. The bed creaked loudly.

What of it? Plenty of people here are buying gold

and want to get away with the Germans toward Vienna. But I'll stay, and so will you, Martyniak. Somebody must get on with the work. We haven't given in to the Germans and we won't give in to the Russians. And we've got America behind us. She won't let them do any harm to us."

Again the story of those years was being repeated. Martyniak looked at Borkowski and saw him in a different light. Now he felt no respect for his energy. He was astonished that he had been in his power for so long. To hell with people like him. He wanted to get up and spit, but instead he sat quietly and listened.

"You, Martyniak, are the man we need. I know you'll agree. You took an oath. You've been a good soldier. The country needs you today."

Martyniak asked:

"So when do we start, sir? Now? At once?"

"As soon as possible. And once we've a place for the printing press, we'll find the machines. Where I am staying it can't be done. Not even room for another pin. Where Polutek lives there are fifty people in one house."

Martyniak let his eyes glide across the rough boards of the floor.

"Well, I'll look around then. Perhaps here, perhaps in some other place. If I find anything, I'll let you know. Where can I find you, sir?"

Borkowski gave him his address and insisted, as he always had done, that he should repeat it.

When he had seen him off and closed the gate behind him, Martyniak went up to his sister-in-law. She stopped digging.

"Who was that? What did he want?"

91

"Oh, some man from Warsaw. But what I was going to tell you is this. I think I'll be going away. To Czestochova, to Theophile's place."

"Starting your plotting again, I suppose. You can never leave well enough alone."

"There's no plot at all. If this man comes here again when I'm away, just tell him I went out and got caught by the Germans in a roundup. If he keeps on calling here, it mightn't be too healthy for you."

20

WITH HIS MIND'S eye Seal saw a confused desert landscape with cliffs rising sharply that quivered with the throbbing in his temples. He was shaken by fever but his wounds were light; the bullet had torn only a piece of skin from his arm. All his efforts were directed at keeping close to Michael and not letting him out of his sight. What had separated them didn't matter now; Michael's unshaven face, the drops of sweat on his forehead, his torn jacket, were the only things he could cling to. The streets in which they found themselves were rows of battered ruins where a human mass swarmed, driven by the tightening circle of battle.

They learned that the attempt to break through to the center of the city, begun two days before, had failed; and the order had been given to leave the Old City by the sewers. This operation was underway. The drive of his previous desire to get there had suddenly returned, as though the gears had meshed again. He no longer had a clear picture of what had happened; he knew only that it was horrible, that from now on he had to do everything in his power to obliterate it, to wipe it from his memory. Only Catherine remained unchanged, untouched by what had happened, and only she could help him. As if from far away he could hear Michael's voice: "Patience. Our turn is coming. Everybody can't leave at once."

The notion of absurdity, of misfortune and chaos was so strong that while dragging himself along behind Michael, he felt it within himself like a sickness. Why did he have to be here? For what purpose? But he stood next to Michael when thin, crazy-eyed women in tattered rags of clothes shook their fists at them: "Criminals! Child-killers! They've left us to be killed and now they're running away themselves!" A stone thrown at him cut his lips and he wiped his mouth clumsily, licking away the salty taste. He didn't protect his head with his arm when a second stone flew past his head. "Yes, I am a criminal. I am, I am," he repeated and there was some solace in it, the reaching of rock bottom: in sordidness and horror everything had become the same, had ceased to be individual.

They were being sent to the northern barricade. But there, among explosions and flying blocks of stone, the same crowd caught up with them, indifferent now to danger. Lugging bundles tied with rope, carrying children, dirty shapeless multitudes—coming from God knew where, from somewhere underground—waved white rags. "Let us pass. We're going over to the Germans."

Voices were raised. "You've tortured us long enough. We're getting out of this hell."

A young boy in a torn coat, a leather belt around

his waist, stood at the foot of the barricade. He tried to make himself heard: "Listen to me! Come to your senses. You'll let the Germans in." They shouted him down: "They're going to slip into the sewers and leave us here! Don't listen to them. They're liars, murderers! Go ahead! Don't ask their permission!" The commander, an officer with graying hair, was brandishing his pistol. He fired it into the air and the sound was lost in the noise of battle. In no time the crowd surrounded them, pieces of rubble in their hands. "Pull down the barricade!" a man's voice shouted. They began frantically to tear down the flagstones and throw them as far away as they could, pushing back the defenders. The young soldiers scattered in all directions, frightened by these infuriated women. The anger of mother, obedience to mother, a blow from mother's hand. Seal heard, "The Germans are coming!" as he stood next to Michael and the commander. On top of the barricades a tangle of hands, heads, white canvas sacks being thrown from one place to another. The commander said: "Oh Jesus" and then in an utterly different voice, "Clear the barricade! Fire! At them!" Michael leveled his submachine gun. Seal heard: "Fire!" He pressed the trigger; the Sten gun vibrated in his hands, and he thought: "Let it happen, I'm a criminal." He was running behind Michael, climbing the barricade, jumping over the convulsively moving arms of a woman, a strip of white skin, a strip of old sunburn. From somewhere rose the wail of a small girl: "Mummy, Mummy!" Behind them were the entrances to the sewers, and other men; the defense had to be continued at all costs. He was firing stubbornly, with one thought: "If I'm killed now, will it be to defend those who are leaving, or my own hope that I shall get away too?"

Many hours later, Michael said, after some discussion with the commander, "Come on. I think we can make it now." The posts were being manned by other men like themselves, grim, dirty, silent. As Michael's group set out, Seal's tongue felt dry like a stiff foreign body in his mouth; there was no water anywhere. On the stairs of the house in which those waiting their turn were collecting, he leaned against a wall and fell asleep. When he opened his eyes he saw Michael holding the hand of a woman wearing a steel helmet. So he had found his wife. More hours passed. In his sleep he heard explosions, the buzz of voices, calls, groans. "The Germans are pouring burning oil into the sewers," somebody next to him said. "Our men have turned back, they couldn't get through."

Michael shook him: "Come on, get ready, our turn now." A slightly built girl in wet overalls, her face smeared with mud, stood near a breach in the wall that gave access to the street. She carried a flashlight on her breast. Strands of curly black hair stuck to her forehead. "I'll lead the way. Don't push. Leave one by one. Crawl quickly. The ditch is screened with flagstones." She produced a cigarette, lit it, inhaled once and then a second time, threw it down, and trod on it. "The Germans are at the entrances further along. There must be absolute silence. If anybody makes a noise he'll kill himself and everybody else."

It took a long time. They got ready, Michael pushed his wife in front of him, but again they had to give way to others. The ditch leading from the house to the sewer entrance was quite shallow. A boy was crawling along it on his back, dragging a wounded comrade; a second boy helped him, moving along on all fours and lifting the wounded man by his belt. Bullets rattled against the broken flagstones which shielded them. 'Wouldn't it be better to stand up in the ditch and get it over with?" Seal asked himself and knew that the answer was no, that he could never do it, because escape from here was an escape from the horrors inside. All of it was bound up with this place; over there in the center he would be a different being: his clean suit hung in a wardrobe, his old life was waiting for him. They're dragging a wounded man; they don't know that he, here, had left Gdula, Joanna, Bertrand behind. The Germans had probably found Gdula and fired a burst into his back. No, Gdula couldn't survive anyhow. So now I'm trying self-justification? "Michael," he said with dry lips. Michael was pushing his wife. "What is it? Don't talk. Come on."

The sun, a crash and chaos of a crumbling world. He was wallowing in the yellow clay of the ditch; he had almost reached the entrance; from down below Michael called: "Don't step on my fingers," and suddenly there was semidarkness and silence. He was lowering himself on iron rungs, yard by yard, into the depths, into safety; the bright circle of the entrance was growing smaller; it was like the discovery of an unknown dimension; silence rang in his ears. Slowly his eyes became accustomed to the darkness. Far inside the tunnel shone the flashlight of the guide. Somebody was holding a candle, its rays feebly lighting the damp walls and the human figures with bent heads. The ceiling was so low that he couldn't stand straight. Water splashed beneath him, soaked into his shoes, and chilled his whole body. "Holy Mother of God, let us get through safely," somebody prayed aloud.

At last the slow march forward began. The gurgling of water, heavy breathing, grunts, the noise of people stumbling against each other, all multiplied by a muffled echo. They were passing some lateral exits, penetrating further and further into the maze under the surface of the city. The fear of the unknown was with them like the fear of travelers in a black, silent, virgin forest. They remembered stories of men who had tried to escape through the sewers and, after a day and night of blind wandering, had found themselves back where they started or had come out into a street occupied by the Germans. This smell—is it gasoline? The bent neck hurt, feet were slipping, tripping over soft objects under water—corpses of men who had died here, or just abandoned bundles? Everything depended on the guide. The faint light moving in front marked her presence.

Seal bumped into Michael's back. The flashlight in front had been switched off. They were standing motionless. He heard a whisper: "There are Germans above us. Wait your turn. Run under the manhole in twos. Pass it back."

21

THE SMALL CARAFES of vodka between the red and white dahlias were dewy and frosted. Peter Kwinto was surprised that there was ice, and he touched the white tablecloth with pleasure. Nearly every face recalled the almost forgotten days before the war. For this reception Baruga had mobilized most of the writers and artists who had found themselves on this side, in Lublin. They were tense, held themselves stiffly, and threw uneasy glances at the head table, where between Baruga and Pekielski the guests sat, broad-shouldered in their military tunics and wide epaulettes—Russian war correspondents. Peter was trying to detect in the faces of the people present the marks of the past few years: the sharper line of a chin, wrinkles, more often the obliteration of particular traits which had once been jealously cultivated. Just as pre-war poems and pictures were losing the individuality which they had seemed to have at the time, disclosing now only the common characteristics of a certain generation and class and period, so the faces of these men, unprotected by the privilege of money or fame, bore the anonymity of a crowd. Shabby coats or workmen's coveralls buttoned up to the neck helped, as they should, to scale them down, to reveal them for what they really were: people who had managed to survive.

Pekielski began his speech by addressing the Russian visitors. He spoke of the invincible Red Army which had brought liberation and the henceforth eternal alliance of the two nations. Stealthy smiles were appearing here and there, but eyes remained fixed on plates. Pekielski's tone was solemn, the intonation as studied as in a sermon. They seemed to detect in it echoes of his past: he had been a priest, had been defrocked, and had become a militant atheist because this was politically expedient. He gave the toast, everybody drank it, and there was indulgent clapping.

The next to get up was Baruga, in his major's uniform. They listened with attention now, knitting their eyebrows, trying to catch the new formulas. This was something quite different. Baruga was no Pekielski. A lot depended on him. He was navigating skilfully between the conflicting requirements of the Russians and of the dialectically unconditioned Polish intellectuals. For the Poles he had phrases about democracy, the sovereignty of the nation, and a "nonviolent revolution." For the Russians—the heroism of the Soviet soldiers, thanks to which the prophesy that the greatest Slav nation would become the savior of the world could come true. In the middle of his speech he switched into Russian and ended with a toast to Generalissimo Stalin. Everybody stood up and clapped.

The guests responded according to their military rank. The first was a colonel, the correspondent of a Moscow magazine. Jutting out his broad chin, he enumerated the victories of the Red Army and ended each paragraph with the words: "*My moguchi,* we are powerful!" and banged his fist on the table. He has chosen the right tactics, thought Peter. To remind us of their strength is the best policy here. The effect was clearly visible on the faces of the audience: fear and anxiety. A toast, zealous clapping.

The guests finished their speeches, the hum of conversation began, the tension slowly relaxed. But again somebody knocked a fork against a glass. They turned their heads in that direction. Peter remembered that the speaker—an abstract painter—had formerly been right wing. Now, stammering (the decision must have cost him a lot) and blushing, he was proclaiming the devotion of the artists to the cause of reform and revolution. In everybody present an internal struggle was going on: ought he to speak and would it be held against him if he didn't? Peter watched Baruga to see if his face showed inner amazement. But no, he exuded merely a benevolent joviality. He caught Julian Halpern's amused look. One might almost start taking bets. Who would be the next? They looked searchingly at one another; and each new speaker who jumped up above the rows of heads and uttered a few sentences in a strangled voice made a stir and evoked murmured comments. Beside Peter sat Bunievicz, whom everybody called Bunio; he smothered his laughter by taking small gulps of vodka. "They aren't in practice yet. They're trying too hard. They think it's necessary to say something original."

Interest was gradually flagging. Heads warmed by the fumes of alcohol were getting closer to each other, jokes were exchanged, the speakers had to wait much longer now for silence, the cigarette smoke grew thicker and was rising to the light bulbs which, as usual, were flickering because the current was weak. Waiters in grubby white coats were serving plates of

100

meat which, because of the number of troops in the town and the difficulty of getting provisions, was a rare treat. The servility of their gestures only partly masked their disdain.

Peter was facing Korpanou, who was not a guest of honor. He had been in the town for some weeks preparing an album of drawings of Nazi atrocities; making sketches for it in the former concentration camp of Maidanek. He was a smallish man with a gray face, and the color of his skin blended with the color of the hair on his upper lip. His military tunic with the badges of rank of a lieutenant of the Red Army could not change his civilian appearance. He was sitting with bowed head, deep in thought, getting up, clapping, pretending to drink, with the same absent expression. Looking at him, Peter had a feeling of guilt. A few days before he had met Korpanov in the street. They spoke for a few moments in Russian and Korpanov touched with his finger the book which Peter was holding under his arm. "What is it? Can I see it?" Peter made a gesture as though he wanted to press the book tighter. "Oh, it's nothing of interest," he said. "Poetry." And at once handed the volume to Korpanov. He noticed his bitter smile and realized that he had hurt him. Our poetry, our Latin alphabet, that's of no interest to Russians; don't interfere in our affairs. Korpanov opened the book and looked at it with the interest of an expert. "A lovely edition." He took his leave almost at once. Turning to go, Peter knew that the breach would never be healed. Who was Korpanov? Who could know what he thought, what his past was? His paintings had sharp, sickly colors—Gestapo men with horsewhips, the specters of prisoners in striped uniforms, heaped naked corpses in blue, yellow, and green light. A compromise between a desire for expression and the photographic style of Soviet illustrations. Hypocrisy, crocodile tears? Peter remembered the Urals. But he understood—or so it seemed to him —the mechanism of life in Russia too well not to guess from Korpanov's art what strivings were expressed in such devious ways. He remembered his meeting with the first Polish woman he had seen for many years and how he had borrowed a book from her in the country house. That was paid off now. He had behaved to Korpanov as that woman had behaved to him. The ties between him and those from whom, as he believed, he had cut himself off, were still strong and their reactions were still the same.

He drank as much as the others, trying to drown his disgust and troubled by a doubt that he had any right to feel it. The conduct of these people was debased, because while hating they praised and while praising, hated even more. But could he justify in any way the hatred he felt when he saw the big fist of the Russian colonel hitting the table to emphasize his *"My moguchi"?* How could this contempt for the Russians be explained? National feeling? Could one trust that? Surrender to the forces of tradition? The good country lady's contempt for him, his for Korpanov. An oversimplification of emotions leading to a vacuum, a submission to irrational reflexes. If I think like this, is it not because strength for me is the ultimate

102

reality? And together with all this, a wave of nausea as though from rotten meat.

Flushed faces were bent over plates; the guests were gleefully stuffing themselves and discussing the food and drink they had known before the war. Faces congealed by tension were softened by the pleasures of satiety. Here and there conversations were starting on the favorite subject—the fate of acquaintances and friends. Loud bursts of laughter accompanied the stories. By laughing, he wondered, were they simply showing relief at their own escape?

"Of course, the first prize should go to Leon," he heard. "In September, at Lvov, he died of food-poisoning from mushrooms as the Red Army marched in. Mushroom-poisoning! Such sublime disregard of history! I'd never have thought he had it in him."

He caught familiar names which were connected in his mind with certain events, with certain days, a party, a meeting: ". . . They ordered all the men to dress and get out. Roman ran up to the attic just as he was, in his pajamas. Charles dressed obediently and went downstairs. He lasted nearly three months in Auschwitz." "He always was very orderly and industrious." They laughed. "To Charles's memory." "To his memory." ". . . I told her, I assured her it was a trap. But no, she was stubborn. She might have lived here quietly; her documents were foolproof; no one would have guessed from looking at her that she was Jewish." Suddenly Peter remembered how she looked —a few months before the outbreak of war. She had a part in Thornton Wilder's *Our Town,* an American teen-ager with a turned-up nose, eating ice cream. "She insisted that everybody who'd left with the first lot had got to France, that they were at Vittel, that they'd sent postcards, that they were getting chocolate —cho-co-la-te!" Karcz, the actor was shaking with laughter. "I said she was stupid. She said no; she reckoned there was one chance in a hundred but she'd had enough of that life—it was so deadly boring." "Was she running short of money?" "Of course not! She had plenty. She came to see me, very smart, a new handbag and pigskin shoes. She was bored, that's all. She showed me a Honduran passport. She applied for an exit visa. They finished them off somewhere in Germany." ". . . No, he was never in the ghetto. He died of blood-poisoning, cut himself with a razor blade." ". . . From Auschwitz she was taken to Ravensbrück." But what about those who had disappeared there without trace, who had been less lucky than Peter? They mustn't be mentioned. So henceforth would there be silence, the spontaneity of a festive meal tempered with caution, a secret censorship operating even when one was drunk, tongues wagging only within the limits defined by fear? They knew a lot, and knowing it they behaved like conspirators.

He saw that Julian was engrossed in conversation with a man wearing a military tunic without badges of rank. "His name's Wolin," Bunio told him in a low voice which echoed with malicious enjoyment. "But it's not his real name. Nobody knows anything about his past. They say he fought in Spain. He is one of the people who'll keep us in order. NKVD. He's organizing the Security Department. I've made a date to have a drink with him, naturally." Just then the other man, as if guessing he was being talked about, looked toward them. It was a quick, sober look, insulated from his surroundings. Amongst the smiling mouths, the gesticulating hands, the glasses clinked together in toasts which were dancing before Peter's eyes, the steel-blue eyes which looked at him were as cold and clear as a mountain top. It lasted only a second, but Peter sobered up immediately and felt annoyed at taking part in something on which Wolin was passing judgment.

"I went to him," somebody next to him was saying, "and showed him a requisition on the treasury. One moment, he said, wait a minute. Perhaps I could have your signature, comrade minister, so that I can get the money from the cashiers? No, you don't need this, there aren't any cashiers yet. This is the cashiers' department. And he produced a bulging wallet from his pocket. The treasury in a wallet!" They leaned back, the noisy hilarity went on. Wolin's eyes took in all of them and then again he began to explain something to Julian, weighing his lighter in his palm.

They now spoke predictions. "The fortuneteller wouldn't tell me anything," Bunio stooped over with a disconsolate expression. "She only said: you'll eat in good restaurants until you're eighty." Gajevicz was nodding approval. "Predictions sometimes come true in reverse. Take Thaddeus for instance. We warned him but he kept saying over and over again: 'I'm not afraid of the Gestapo; a fortuneteller told me that I'm going to get married on the thirtieth of May.' He was arrested on the thirteenth and shot on the thirtieth.

105

The woman had mixed up the heart-line and the life-line."

Bunio's laughter at the absurdity of the world had a note of satisfaction in it—satisfaction at the confirmation of a theory. He was rubbing his face, which was covered with dark spots, and drinking vodka from a tumbler. He moved nearer to Peter and said unexpectedly: "You've seen it all already. Now it's being repeated. They'll cringe and play-act. Believe me, I'm not lying. The only thing I know is how to write funny stories and I'll write for anybody who pays me. It's what writers have always done and always will do. And if anybody tells you anything else he's a liar."

Intoxication was now reaching the stage of embraces and mutual admiration. Korpanov, who had been talking to his neighbor about Goya, relapsed into melancholy silence. All round them, people were praising each other's poems and books. "The best novel of the last twenty years!" "I've always said outside of us, there's no literature!" "You can't compare yourself with Tom, his style's appalling." "Johnny, a toast to our survival!" "I drink to the health of the most eminent poet of our day." Somebody was being led out, somebody else was having an argument with the waiter about getting more vodka. On coffee-stained tablecloths, stubs of cigarettes were scattered around full ashtrays.

They were getting up from the tables on shaky legs and walking unsteadily. The cold air of the clear night was too much for Peter; he leaned against a lintel. Groups of chattering people were disappearing

down the empty street. He realized that all through
the reception he had been thinking about what was
happening in Warsaw and that this lay at the root of
his horrible feeling of insecurity and falseness.

He noticed that next to him Korpanov stood alone,
his hands in his pockets, gazing at the stars. He said
to him:

"I don't like banquets."

And applying the acquired method of limited frankness, he at once amplified the statement by saying:

"They're apt to make one forget that the war's
still on."

Korpanov coughed noncommitally.

Part Two

"THE CORCYRAEANS, NOT *liking themselves to force a passage by the doors, got up on the top of the building, and breaking through the roof, threw down the tiles and let fly arrows at them, from which the prisoners sheltered themselves as well as they could. Most of their number, meanwhile, were engaged in dispatching themselves by thrusting into their throats the arrows shot by the enemy and hanging themselves with the cords taken from some beds, that happened to be there, and with strips made from their clothing; adopting, in short, every possible means of self-destruction, and also falling victims to the missiles of their enemies on the roof. Night came on while these horrors were enacting, and most of it had passed before they were concluded. When it was day, the Corcyraeans threw them in layers upon wagons and carried them out of the city. All the women taken in the stronghold were sold as slaves. In this way the Corcy-*

raeans of the mountain were destroyed by the commons; and so after terrible excesses the party strife came to an end, at least as far as the period of this war is concerned, for of one party there was practically nothing left."

Professor Gil put down his pen and sat unmoving. That girl. Her white blouse, red tie; she—one among the thousands of boys and girls whose childhood had coincided with the war years when the shape of their lives and thoughts had been determined. She came to ask what the word "stoical" meant. She needed it for an essay. She lived with a friend in an adjoining room, but Gil saw her only occasionally. All of them were engrossed in essays, work, discipline, meetings, marches with standards and portraits of the leaders. In the social mechanism everything must be paid for: for her, the daughter of a janitor, there were universities, a future. But she would never know the things he himself had once known in his youth, the anxiety to catch an elusive truth which, like a touch, cannot be defined in words. Joanna died fighting against the Nazis but, in fact, barring access to a university for this girl: were it not for the new system, it would perhaps still be as difficult for a janitor's daughter to climb to the surface as it had been for him. And it was immaterial that Joanna did not wish to defend a bad order. Objectively, as one nowadays says, she had defended it. Objectively? He had given her what he could. Years had passed, many years, but the memory had not faded of her arm around his neck as

110

she sat on his knee, a small, serious child, listening to stories about Greek heroes and demigods.

He had given her some idea of the mystery of the world and of the mysteriousness of history; he had told her of the changes in human standards in the face of which the only important things were deeds, for their motives were exposed to the unforeseeable judgment of posterity. He had brought her up to be unceasingly interested in human affairs and in that unknown future which could not be conquered otherwise than by the decisions of each and every moment. He had had his recompense—the happiness of love between father and daughter, of daily mutual confidences about their work and their hopes. If at that time, before the war, he had sent her to Switzerland as he had wanted, this would not have happened. But too many things had united them: her studies, her help with his work. And now, many a time, at night, on the borderline between sleep and wakefulness, he saw the substance of Joanna's body disintegrating in the ground, a small slim skeleton receding into the past ages of mankind. Thucydides. "After terrible excesses the party strife came to an end. . . ."

Standards. He knew what the girl in the white blouse and red tie was thinking about him: a funny old professor without a position, a harmless reactionary who could safely be left alone, a man who did not understand the greatness of the new era. He had some bourgeois wisdom which one can make use of, but with due care. Ideas die away for long years, as they did in the twilight of Greece; when taken up anew and

111

revived, they are never the same, they have been changed by the flow of the Heraclitean river. What had been in him or in Joanna would return some time, changed. But he would be unable to explain anything to this girl. She would not understand if he told her that the new world in which she believed was a cruel world because it lacked respect for the complexity of man, respect which perhaps ought to be called piety. She would not understand either, if he expressed doubts about what was at present the basis of education: belief in science and its ability to reveal the absolute truth of history. Marx, the bearded iconoclast, the destroyer of absolute truths, the admirer of Aeschylus, would never have thought that generations would march under his sign in disciplined cohorts, persuaded by those in power that full knowledge had at last become the heritage of the human species—knowledge absolute and full because backed by power, which, according to that same knowledge, was the ultimate corroboration of the validity of that knowledge: à vicious circle conceived by Hegel's genius. In four or five hundred years, perhaps it would be possible again to greet the word Weltgeist with a smile of pity. But before that happened the sense of pity was going to perish; there would only be blind faith adorned with scientific trappings. Perhaps it was time for a return to fanaticism. If all these young people were as happy as that girl, did we have any right to deprive them of their certainty, to stir up the storms that slept, unknown to them, in their hearts?

Contempt was difficult to bear. People like himself were treated with contempt, and he had to accept this.

112

*Not only that: the term "petty-bourgeois mentality"
embraced all those who did not acquiesce completely
—both himself and those whom he thought of as
enemies. In the first years after the war, when he had
not yet learned how to endure solitude, he would call
on people he knew who, like himself, had settled in
this ruined city whose German population had been
driven away. Over cups of coffee and pastry, their
faces flushed, they would exchange the latest news
heard over foreign radio stations and tell malicious
stories about the Bolshevik government. Their pitiful
stupidity—and the stupidity of the whole doomed
caste they represented—made him feel guilty: these
were the people responsible for the social order before
the war, for everything he hated. He could never forget that he had been humiliated in his youth by such
people; the son of a peasant from Galicia, he had
made his way through the university by the sheer
force of his vitality and perseverance, without any
social graces, not knowing what to do with his hands.
Later, he became one of them, a professor. And now
he was one of those who resisted. To join them would
mean preserving the fiction of belonging to them and
all they represented. So he had broken off all relations,
had stopped visiting anybody. But the connection with
them still remained, imposed by those in power: you
could only be for or against. Nuances meant nothing.*

*His university colleagues proclaimed, one after the
other, their adherence to the principles of Marxism-
Leninism-Stalinism. They were prompted to do so not
simply by the desire to preserve their chairs. They
could not stand contempt; they began to feel that if*

113

they resisted, it was because, without admitting it to themselves, their decision was predetermined by allegiance to their own class. To avoid the fall—shameful in their eyes—into the abyss where the dispossessed recalled the good old days and waited for the Americans to come was possible only if one accepted orthodoxy completely. They were encouraged in this, and the transition was made gradual, painless, easy.

The girl in the white blouse and red tie was closer to Gil than the students with whom, before the war, he had shaken hands and exchanged pleasantries. In this instance, his dream was fulfilled: the universities were thrown open to the sons and daughters of peasants and workers. And yet not entirely fulfilled, because for its fulfillment a supreme price must be paid.

Outside the window the clock on the scarred Gothic tower was striking the hour. Gil did not like the city. It had been burned in 1945 by the Red Army when it besieged the Germans there and the whole of the center was still a mass of ruins. He went for walks along the banks of the canals, striding through the desolation which in both spring and autumn was a patchwork of withered grass, of rusty iron fences, of crumbling bricks. Here, near this city, his wife had died soon after their release from the camp to which they had been deported from Warsaw. At that time he bore it almost with indifference; he was weak and thought that for him, too, it was only a matter of days. But typhus had spared him. It was from here, later on, that he had started to search for Joanna; he had returned to these ruined streets, without being quite sure why, unless it was because he had to return somewhere.

114

Decisions? But all developed almost automatically. When lecturing he spoke of things in which he believed: that the perspective in which historical events are seen is continuously changing and that the past, like the poor shadows of Hades, revives only when it is fed on the blood of the living. The past of Greece was resuscitated in different ways all the time and each time it served to support the theses dictated by the idiosyncrasies of historians. He tried to explain to his students how the search for truth was exposed to many dangers, how faint and, at the same time, how splendid was its light—the light of a candle blown out over and over again by the wind. He did not hesitate to speak of Marx. If, as Marx maintained, truth was a weapon in the class war then, when a new society was formed and the necessity for this war had disappeared, perhaps a new vision of life would be given to men?—His removal from his chair was polite. The reason given was not the age limit—fifty-eight was too young for that—but his need for prolonged rest after the hardships of the concentration camp. Once again, as so many times before, he asked himself a question: was the decision in any way his and did he really anticipate losing his chair, or had he overlooked the possibility of such an occurrence, attaching too much importance to the short period of relative liberalism? To find an answer was most important, but it was impossible to find it.

"Undermining the belief in the capacity of the human mind to acquire knowledge. Spreading of bourgeois agnosticism and objectivism," such, he knew, was the diagnosis of his sickness. The borderline between the adherents of a belief in the relativity of moral

115

and intellectual judgments, whom he considered to be the scourge of the twentieth century, and those, who, like himself, tried to remove the falsehoods blocking the road to knowledge, was willfully obscured by those in authority. But the nobility of one's own motives was questionable. To be separated from those girls and boys in red ties meant separation from life; no matter what kind of life—simply life. Isolation, whether he wanted it or not, was already destroying him; the words which could not be given life, the common abortion of his ideas was poisoning him inwardly. And they, having created conditions under which they had to be right, were right: whoever was against them was simply moving backwards; whoever wanted to advance had to adopt the new religion.

Had he remained faithful to Joanna? Her death was physical; a stopping at a definite point in time. But he, although trying to remain what he had been, had changed. One cannot with impunity defy the whole rhythm of one's surroundings. When he had left his native village for the city, eager to fight for progress, he did not expect that one day he would suffer a defeat like this.

He felt a chill; these springs were long drawn out and sunless. He pulled at his sweater and noticed that he still hadn't remembered to ask for thread to sew a button on. He reached for his pen: "Meanwhile the Athenians sailed off to Sicily, their primary destination, and carried on the war with their allies there."

Towards the Elbe

1

IT WAS ALREADY April when Peter Kwinto arrived in Warsaw in a jeep. The suburb of Praga looked just as he had known it before the war. Dirty tenement houses with warping wooden structures between them, long straight streets paved roughly with cobblestones, wind—there was always wind here—sweeping up spirals of sand and litter. Only the lopped-off towers of St. Florian's and occasional shrapnel-scarred walls reminded one of the war. All the same, Praga had changed. Its main street was transformed into a bazaar and camping site. Soviet girls, blouses bulging with their heavy breasts, were directing traffic: military trucks, jeeps, rusty cars which used to be taxis, rickshaws, handcarts; the crowd: Soviet infantrymen, tank crews, NKVD men, women in shawls, in skiing boots, with rucksacks, shabby civilians with bundles, Polish soldiers—everybody milling about, buying and selling shirts, tires, canned goods, rolls of cloth, vodka, accordions, trousers, radios, half-burned books—treasures collected from the ruins on the other side of the river or looted in Germany. Sentries stood in the gateways of certain buildings for the new government had moved to the capital and was housing its newly organized departments in the small apartments of this working-class suburb. The streets shook with noise. Trucks drew up at the curb, and clusters of boys acted as barkers for the drivers: "Going any minute now! Going any minute now! Warsaw only twenty zloty per person!"

Peter's driver was cursing. The street leading to the city was choked with a column of vehicles; they crawled slowly forward, then stopped dead, then started again for a moment: it seemed as if they would have to wait for hours. Peter amused himself by watching what was happening in front: he saw the open back of a truck loaded with tires. A Soviet soldier tried to climb on the truck, slipped and fell back, his movements as clumsy as in a slow-motion film. At last he got on and tried to roll one of the tires off; but he was too drunk; he fell across the tire, which looped over him: with great effort he was enacting what seemed a grotesque circus parody of an unsuccessful theft.

They reached the river. Ragged spring clouds, wind across an open space, pillars of ruined bridges. Gulls circled with shrill cries over the mud flats. On the other side, in the cold sunshine, they could see the uneven line of the ruins. Their color for some unknown reason reminded him of meat—horsemeat; it was an absurd notion, for in fact they were shades

120

lighter. Peter screwed up his eyes and tried to recognize the buildings he had known. But he could not make any out; there was only a chaos of battered walls, gaping holes, and great diagonal cracks. Only the fourteen-story building in Napoleon Square stood out above this irregular range; it had lost all its old elegance and looked like a half-chewed corncob. They crossed by the wooden bridge; it swayed and shook, carrying much too heavy a load, but it was the only means of crossing the river; it had been built by Soviet sappers. On the other side, the enormous faces of members of the new government, clumsily painted on wooden boards, looked down at them from tall poles. Trucks filled with masses of standing women and men hanging onto one another in order to keep upright— they looked like they were embracing each other— bumped along, turned, and disappeared into the backdrop of debris. People on foot, loaded with pieces of furniture, with bundles and suitcases held by leather straps, walked laboriously up the sloping road between the vehicles.

Peter did not quite know where to go. There were no addresses, no faces, no telephones—nothing but streets. And even these hardly existed. In their place ran narrow paths made by the feet of people returning to their homes and by the tracks of military vehicles. The jeep kept skidding against piles of debris, which rose to what must once have been second-floor level. Brick dust grated between his teeth. The sweet, sickly smell of corpses, warmed by the spring weather, hung in the air in layers. As they neared the streets where he had lived before the war, they ran into barricades

121

that had not yet been pulled down. Peter left the jeep and continued on foot.

The paving stones were all torn up. In the sand stood hurriedly nailed wooden crosses. Some people in small groups were busy digging. They had handkerchiefs tied round their noses and mouths. Women were kneeling at the edges of the holes, looking down. At one of them Peter stopped to look. A bundle of old rags, the contorted outline of a body decomposing into a dirty mess with only the fair, sandy hair untouched by destruction. Long furrows on the woman's face, tears falling slowly. Antigone, still searching across the centuries for her Polynices. Now they'll lay these bones on a sheet and carry it by the edges. Resuming his walk, Peter inhaled his cigarette deeply to drown the persistent stench.

Silence. Through the unshapely gaps in these battered, weather-beaten rocks, the blue sky. There were no birds, he noticed. He stopped in front of the house where he had lived; it had survived almost whole but it was gutted. The courtyard was pitted with bomb craters and there were graves where the lawn had been. A steel helmet lay on one of them. Standing in the middle of the yard, he looked up at the empty windows. It was then that he noticed the smoke. It was seeping from a tin pipe which jutted out low down on the wall. People had moved in again. An old man with a walrus mustache came from the cellar, dragging behind him some bent pieces of iron. He looked at Peter with indifference.

"What has happened to the people who used to live in this house? Are you from here?" Peter asked.

He knew that his mother was alive, living in the country near Warsaw. But he had known many people here, followed their daily affairs, and taken an interest in their lives.

"I'm from number ten. I didn't know the people here. My wife might. She used to come here as a cleaner."

The old woman looked at Peter as if he were an inanimate object. What was the matter with them all? They themselves looked like the burned-out skeletons of houses. They possessed the calm of devastation.

"Do you know what happened to Mr. Krajevski? He used to live on the first floor."

"Krajevski?" She was trying hard to remember. "Yes, there was somebody of that name. But he didn't come back after '39. They said he was in England."

"And Gontar?"

"Him I knew. Nothing certain. Dachau. His wife and daughters lived here but they were killed."

"Did you know Martyniak?"

"That printer? He left. The Gestapo was looking for him."

"And what happened to the Urbanskis?"

Peter used to like to call at Urbanski's workshop, which was in the courtyard on the ground floor. The regular rhythm of the plane, the smell of wood, the muscular hands touching the boards with knowledge and skill: Urbanski loved his job. When he received a new design for a table or a couch, he would discuss it with Peter, wetting a thick carpenter's pencil with his tongue and putting fat, straight lines on paper. As he wielded his plane or a saw, he would chatter incessantly. He told tales and legends of his native region, the inaccessible forest country on the borders of East Prussia. His wife's hair was flaxen and her eyes were black; their three small daughters were exactly like her. Whenever Peter went to see them at night, she would put tea in front of him and sit quietly knitting, only lifting her eyes from time to time, quick, understanding, showing that she had been listening and had her own opinion about most things.

"Urbanski. Oh, that was a long time ago. They arrested him in the street, back in '40. He died at Auschwitz. His wife and daughters—they, like nearly everybody else here . . ." She paused.

"What do you mean, like nearly everybody else here?"

The old woman pointed with her finger at the ground.

"They said this house was unsafe. Weak, wouldn't stand up to bombing. So nearly everybody went to number sixteen, to the cellar of that big house. Then there was a direct hit and they were buried alive. They're still there. There's nobody to dig them out. It would take months."

Walking in the middle of the road, Peter recognized the place from a distance. A great heap of broken walls. He realized now that he had remembered Mrs. Urbanski's eyes more than once during his wanderings. The soft circle of lamplight and the quick glances of that quiet woman. A symbol of all that was being destroyed. An evening with a contented family after a day's work. Had Mrs. Urbanski's eyes been for him a signal from home, a symbol of Poland itself? He was right to have come to Warsaw. He took off his military cap and stood still, thinking of the sufferings of the dying.

2

MAJOR BARUGA WAS walking along a street in Praga towards the offices of the Central Committee of the Party. A few yards behind him walked a tall boy in a military cape, with an automatic weapon slung across his breast. Baruga did not like to admit to himself his concern for his own safety; even less did he like to admit it to others. He had given in to the entreaties of his mistress and taken on a bodyguard. A few months before, at Lublin, Baruga had saved him from arrest when he was in danger along with everyone else who had served in the Home Army. Frightened and suspicious of the terrible Bolsheviks, this child wanted only to be left in peace. Baruga gave him a corner in his house where he could sleep and allowed him to listen as often as he liked to the discussions and arguments that were so much a part of his daily work as Director of Publications. It was the best way. Gradually, after the boy had begun to ask him timid questions, he had talked to him seriously a number of times. The lad became attached to him and developed a faithful, almost doglike devotion. He made an admirable bodyguard. Boys like this were a source of pride to Baruga. He considered a talent for teaching a necessary accomplishment for a good Communist. Moreover, these people whom he

125

was leading out of the savage wilderness of the war years and who treated him as a great man, were a true fulfillment of his ambitions.

He inhaled the spring air deeply. The grandiose scale of recent events and the fact that he was walking here, in the streets of that city—destroyed yet already belonging to the future, to a new humanity—intoxicated him. If only life would last long enough for the almost infinite number of things there were to be done. Some way must be discovered of lengthening the span of human life. And supposing he had emigrated to Venezuela before the war, as he had wanted to do in a moment of doubt when it had seemed to him that fascism would win? The wrong decision at one moment can bring misfortune for the rest of one's life. What would he have been now? He would have had to return here on bended knee, whining that he had been a coward, that he had made a mistake.

The stairs of the building housing the Central Committee were dirty, covered with spit and stamped out cigarette butts. Doors slammed; there was the murmur of voices. When he had given his name to an individual whose muscles bulged under a black coat much too tight for him, he did not have long to wait.

The Secretary General got up from behind his desk and limped a few paces toward him. Before the war he had been shot in the legs by warders while escaping from prison. His big proletarian face was very tired. Only his eyes, dark and intense, gave it some life. The yellow tinge of the skin, the bald, domed forehead, and the mouth surrounded by deep furrows made him look like a gnome. Baruga sank heavily

126

into an armchair whose arms were spilling their stuffing. His double chin rested on the high collar of his uniform tunic and the scar of an old goiter operation was visible.

"We've discussed the situation. That's why I'm here today with a concrete proposition. Everything's bound up with it. We're quite ready to hang up a notice saying: 'Whoever's against our present tactics, is against all tactics.'"

He was breathing heavily. The Secretary General offered him an open cigarette case, took a cigarette himself, and snapped the case shut. He nodded. Baruga unbuttoned his collar, which was cutting his neck.

"It's very clear. You understand it because you've been here inside the country all through the most difficult period. But when there are tanks on the other side, not to dig trenches and not to lay traps is not a proof of courage. It's just nonsense. Unfortunately, we're passing through a phase like 1917 in Russia, even if it's on a much smaller scale. And we've got our tactics cut and dried."

The Secretary General was smoking nervously and biting through the paper tip of his Russian cigarette; a vertical wrinkle appeared between his eyebrows.

"I've created a press for you," Baruga said, not pronouncing his r's. "And I'll continue to keep a press going as long as the Party wants me to. But I need help. And sometimes I have to appeal to you and the other comrades. I'm doing as much as I can by myself."

"You know you're irreplaceable," said the Secretary.

"They've taken the cook at my canteen for the

127

Polish Socialist Party. In the little shop around the corner," Baruga snorted with laughter, "and in all the other little shops they're recruiting new members. Let's assume that all the leaders of the Socialist right wing are either dead or have escaped. Now all the scum are rushing to join the Socialists because theirs is a pat-ri-o-tic party and at the same time legal. Meanwhile, I've got to keep anybody who can think or write away from the Peasant Party."

The gnome behind the desk waved his hand disdainfully. Baruga leaned forward in his armchair.

"But that's not what matters. What matters is that there are too few counter-irritants. The fact that this city," he pointed to the window, "is in ruins is a psychological factor against us and a very powerful one at that. The decision to transfer the seat of government here to Praga was absolutely right. But the effect won't be felt till later. There's the whole burden of the past to reckon with. And besides, they're killing our men."

The Secretary General said, without lifting his eyes:

"A balance must be maintained between necessary intimidation and temporary concessions."

Baruga's face reddened. Such a qualification, on the part of this supporter of a "national front" and addressed to him, was proof of overcautiousness. He said hoarsely:

"So far as I'm concerned, you understand, this isn't a concession to the class enemy. My job's to keep an eye on the psychological climate. Our methods of molding consciousness are almost unlimited. Unlimited. That's the aim of terror. Across the chasm—

128

excuse the clichés—footbridges must be built at points which suit us. And they'll have to use those bridges because they're frightened. If there's no other way out, they'll go to the forests."

The Secretary General asked, looking towards the window:

"But you must surely understand the necessities of the present moment? Have I got to remind you that the war's still going on."

Again the same move. He's shielding himself, implying that I'm given to fantasies, thought Baruga. He answered lazily:

"Collective methods form the necessary background. By them you can create fear. Myself, I'm only a propagandist. I'm interested in footbridges and, for the moment, in a concrete plan."

The gnome shot a penetrating glance at him:

"I may, of course, be wrong," continued Baruga, "but it seems to me that I'm being consistent where Comrade Lampe's program is concerned. We've learned not to treat nationalism lightly. Or religion, for that matter."

Thinking he had startled him (these purists drive one to drink; they're always lagging behind; the only instrument they understand's the left wing, Baruga added quickly:

"The attitude of the Politburo is unequivocal. During the next few years, tactics will lead in that direction everywhere. We have a difficult country, and as yet we have done too little."

The Secretary General fiddled with the ashtray. Baruga's opening remarks were always the same.

"I'm making a suggestion. Of course, it will have to be approved. I shall put it before the comrades. It would be possible, if you wish, to start a special paper which would help lower the temperature. The Catholic and nationalist front is neglected. We should provide an outlet for their feelings and create a group among them that we can keep under our own control. I should like your views on this. If you think it's a good idea, I'd like your support."

"What exactly have you in mind?"

"I don't know if you've been told. The Soviet Security has approached us with a proposal. They believe that a bird they've caught could be useful to us. Of course," Baruga shrugged, "we needn't take advantage of their suggestion. You'll know the name: Michael Kamienski."

The Secretary General jumped to his feet. He pushed his hands deep into his pockets and limped around the room with the halting step of a cripple. He reminded Baruga of the tailor who had made suits for him before the war, a poor emaciated wretch sitting at his bench, his legs broken in a childhood accident.

"That ideologist of fascism and anti-Semitism? The blackest reactionary in the country? So we arrest stupid children of the Home Army and let him go free? What are we coming to?"

Baruga said coldly:

"He's got a name. That means something. And he fought in the rising, in the Old City. Fought well, too. Our friends have realized his worth. Otherwise they wouldn't have wasted time on him. We might get him. He would bring in other birds of the same feather."

The Secretary sat down and asked violently:

"So that one more person may practice Machiavellism, while awaiting the return of more favorable circumstances?"

Baruga laughed gutturally:

"Not exactly. You must excuse me—metaphors are my little weakness: though a fly may touch flypaper only for a moment, the flypaper has caught it all the same. First they cheat us, then themselves, then they get lost in the double game. Psychological transformations are inevitable. We hold the key."

The Secretary's mouth was twisted in a bitter smile:

"What a nation! Wherever you look only fascists, nationalists, priest-ridden fanatics, gamblers. I envy the Yugoslavs—millions of loyal, reliable people. We have to build with dung."

It's true what people say: he can't adapt himself to power, Baruga said to himself. There must be some reason for this rigid revolutionary attitude. Probably identification with his own slogans or inadequate intellectual training.

The Secretary said sorrowfully:

"Of course, I recognize the need for diversionary action. I agree that one must isolate the groups and deal with them one by one. But I'm afraid it may be a double-edged weapon. I would like to hear what the other comrades think of it."

Baruga was pleased. The Secretary had to reckon with him, and even if he was now displaying this noble sorrow, that was enough. Moreover, Baruga had the backing of personalities more important than the Secretary General. Everything was clear. The same thing would have to be done, sooner or later, in all the liberated countries. Besides, he wouldn't have done anything had it not been for his conversation with Tukhanov.

"I've something for you," the Secretary was turning the pages of a diary lying on the table. "Here it is. Reports about a paper mill in the Western Territories. At Eichenberg. We must save it. Speed's essential. Have you anyone you can trust?"

The snatching of plants from under the Russians' noses. One more inner conflict of a pure revolutionary. Where will it all lead him in the end? He answered:

"Of course. Thank you for the information. I'll find someone at once and send him to you."

"He must be a Party member and resourceful. I don't want anyone who's liable to get cold feet."

Walking heavily downstairs, Baruga mentally reviewed the matters he still had to deal with that day. What was the average span of human life in the Middle Ages? Probably forty, fifty years. Ridiculous. A man ought to live for three hundred, four hundred years. But what if science lagged behind in this revolutionary passage from prehistory to conscious history molded by reason? The barrenness of old age? Quite unacceptable.

He stopped and waited until the boy in the military cape came up.

"Remember this. The seed from which a tree will grow is tiny and no one can guess the shape of the tree from it. You'll be telling your grandchildren about the year 1945."

3

WHAT A RELIEF it was when there was no longer any need to be on the defensive. Peter clasped his hands behind his head and looked at his mother from under half-closed lids. It was just as in his childhood when he had had the flu; illness was a break in the course of passing time. Now his mother was sitting at his bedside, stirring his tea, which she had put on the little table. The reunion had been embarrassing. Her tears, her unchecked show of emotion reminded him of those times in the past when he had been ashamed of her, or rather ashamed of himself, while discovering in her the same physical traits and the same apparent excitability that he himself possessed. He did not know if such feelings of shame was characteristic of all relations between children and parents. Perhaps parents always looked to their children like caricatures of certain traits and qualities of their own. Or perhaps this was unique to his relation with his mother. Yet now, when she was next to him, simply existing, he again could return to the past, to simple happiness, to security.

His mother's hands were knotted with rheumatism. Her cheekbones were even more prominent than before —the cheekbones he had inherited from her. She had worn badly—her face, always younger-looking than her years, was beginning to crumple now, was losing its elasticity without gaining any new harmony. Her dark dress had been mended in many places. He remembered that dress. Now it was the only one she possessed: she had worn it when she left Warsaw to spend a few days here in the country, and the rising had started meanwhile. Her throat was working as if she were swallowing unspoken words. Her only child was alive, had been returned to her. They had already told each other everything that had happened to them during these last few years. The fact that they had found each other was a miracle.

"Drink this, it will do you good. I put some dried raspberries in it. I'd like to give you an aspirin, but there aren't any." She handed him the cup. "People are unkind. The doctor's wife has said some nasty things already about your uniform. But I know your father wouldn't have blamed you. Things are so frightful now."

Peter drank the tea and thought about the unattainable longing of his life. He remembered his father only as something large and warm, an emanation of cheerful strength, a great knotty tree embracing him with its branches. His father was killed in military action when Peter was six. Bourgeois Europe was, within its limited powers, trying at the time to do something to combat the threat it saw in the Russian Revolution. Up to a point it succeeded. It was unable to overthrow the Bolsheviks, but their advance was checked by the Battle of Warsaw. Were it not for this, Peter's upbringing would have been different and he would not have experienced so many conflicts. But who knows? He would not have experienced many other things either, good and bad. By making him an orphan, his father left him a blind aspiration, a childish crying for something which was too unreal to be defined. Owing to his death, Peter, like so many others, had attended a school in which a lot had been said about Western civilization, about countries that were *antemurale christianitatis,* where Latin was considered to be one of the most important subjects and Russian was not among the foreign languages taught. Twenty-four years had gone by since Soviet shrapnel killed his father. He had been more or less the same age as Peter was now. Today his defeat was complete. *Antemurale christianitatis* was becoming the *antemurale* of a new faith. Yet the time bought by his father's death counted for something. Different chemical combinations had emerged, different courses of human destiny, a different general balance. One could not say whether his father had had a foretaste of present-day conflicts. They were only just beginning at the time. Maybe he did. Like Pilsudski, a fearless revolutionary in his youth who, when he became a dictator, said of himself that he had stopped for a short time the wheel of history.

"Peter my child, tell me what's going to happen. They're so terribly hated by our people. We prayed for liberation and liberation has come—in the shape of a new occupation. They'll make Poland another one of their republics."

Peter put down his cup and, pulling the blanket up to his chin, enjoyed the warmth spreading all over his body. Simultaneously with the warmth, the presence of his mother and the circle of lamplight, he was con-

135

scious of what was happening outside the house. He had gone out for a moment in the afternoon, wearing a windbreaker he had bought in Praga: there was no sense in parading around in uniform here and attracting hostile glances. The unpaved street of the summer resort was empty. Crooked pine trees towered over the dunes of loose sand. Clouds were sailing slowly across the dark sky. A small boy crouching on his heels was moving a wooden toy car backwards and forwards, murmuring to himself. He was thin and pale, his bare knees were blue with cold, and he was wearing a shabby coat. Peter crouched beside him and asked him where he lived. The child, not lifting his head, pointed to a little red brick house on the bare dune. "I live there with Mummy." "Haven't you got a daddy?" "My daddy's in hiding. He sometimes comes at night." Peter stroked the boy's fair hair. He continued on his way with bowed head. Everywhere the same thing. These years had taught even the children to consider "being in hiding" something natural. At the same time, the child did not understand that the stranger might be dangerous. Peter looked like a father and spoke Polish.

"I know," his mother was saying, "believe me, I feel it. I feel many things. It can't end well. Now they are hanging out these national flags. That's cheating. It will be a bottomless precipice. I had a dream about it."

His mother's dreams and premonitions had always given Peter cause for reflection. While they would be having breakfast, before he went off to school and she to her office, she would tell him her dreams and interpret them for him. Perhaps these were just superstitions. His mother herself treated them only half-seriously, but Peter's intuition, which often helped him get out of difficult situations—while different in quality—did not differ in kind from his mother's irrational beliefs.

"Peter, my darling, you've come through all this unscathed and now you're back home. But I can only give you one piece of advice: escape. Don't think about me. You mustn't start a new life here. I don't need anything now. I'll manage all right. Escape while there's still time."

To escape. In the cattle car taking him to the Urals, that was his dream and that of all his fellow-prisoners. There, in camp, they weighed all the possibilities in whispers: not a chance. They faced the envy of their Russian fellow-sufferers when the amnesty was proclaimed.—Never to have anything more to do with Russia, to get out at any price. Of course, he would have joined the London army. He would have been in the Middle East or in Italy by now. But he was discharged too late, when the Polish Army had already reached Persia. And all his cunning, this walk on a tightrope, had been in the belief that the new Red Army would lead the way to the West. Now here, in his native land, he could observe in himself the conflicting reactions of disgust and anger. And what if everything should be repeated here that had been done over there? To escape anywhere, as far away as possible, to Australia, to work at anything, to forget. Yet this was his country. And what if there was hope, even a glimmer of hope, that something new would emerge here? There would be gradual stages, and the efforts of millions of people like himself. Should he surrender to emotional impulses arising in a moment of chaos, destruction, revolution? Must one plan one's life on the basis of what might happen in five, ten years' time? His mother was expressing his most secret thought. And by doing this, she had revealed to him his own cowardice.

"I don't know, Mama. These are only temporary conditions. Much will change, though not in the way most people here believe. You mustn't count on the West. Everything depends on ourselves. Perhaps a form of socialism is possible. With conditions as they are, they won't be able to digest us so easily."

She smiled pityingly:

"Do you think I don't understand you, my child? I'm stupid, I don't know anything about theories. But you want to convince yourself that what *is* the same won't be the same. For you're better off here than in Russia. Human beings think in terms of places, of regions. Our secret organizations came across letters written by German soldiers on the Eastern front to their families. They cursed the country of murders and atrocities and longed for their net curtains and flower pots and *Gemütlichkeit*. Yet they themselves committed murders and atrocities. The place, the region must have been responsible."

He was groping for words, looking at the boards of the ceiling.

"But what's one to do, Mother, if there's a rock bottom—of poverty, oppression, humiliation—and if

138

it is only by reaching these depths that people can change the world? What surrounded us before the war now seems to me futile, unstable, and shallow. I don't know which is worse—that past or the iron present of the Communists. I'm trying to understand and can't. Over there, they've made a horrible parody of it. And now the whole of Europe lies open to them. One day something new must come out of it."

His mother's mouth hardened:

"What begins with a lie will remain a lie. Your father was overjoyed when the Revolution broke out there. Czarism was abolished. You know yourself what it's like. You talk the way you do because you have to. If you'd spoken differently you wouldn't have been able to get out. Anyone who speaks the way he has to speak begins to think what he's got to think."

No, he hadn't reached that stage yet. But not even to his mother could he disclose the tortuous course of his reasoning, which was like a complicated mechanism, full of intermeshed cogwheels, functioning, it seemed, independently of himself. He felt this mechanism as a foreign body, but at the same time knew that he mustn't rebel against it: his whole hope was centered around the belief that one day he might be able to solve the riddle of its various parts. And the insincerity of words spoken in public and the clear mental processes that at the same time assessed the spoken words as only a fraction of the truth—*was* possible solely because of that hope. It was like a constant pleading for time and more time.

"Don't try to be different from what you are. You're

still the same person, you're my son." His mother was tucking him in. "A mother's prayer sometimes works. Now you must sweat out that nasty cold."

He could hear her moving about, making up her own bed.

He tried to work out the final answer but it eluded him as usual.

"Shall I switch off the light?" his mother asked.

"Good night, Mama," he answered, half asleep already.

4

HERE, NOTHING WAS left standing. An enormous expanse of ruins lay flat in the cold morning light. The shadows of ragged clouds moved across it and little whirlwinds of brick dust rose here and there from the bare mounds between the banks of dead weeds. The wind ruffled Bruno's black hair. He wiped his red nose with a handkerchief and then began carefully to wipe his eyeglasses.

"Look," he said to Peter. "You can understand now what's meant by 'razing to the ground.' Not a trace left. My place was here, yet I wasn't here. Not when they were deported, nor during that desperate rising. And anyone who survived did as I've done: at the price of breaking away."

Peter was silent. He had never imagined that the ruins of the ghetto would be like this. This was the abomination of desolation.

"Over there, on the Aryan side, I died of fear every

140

day. If I'd been caught, I'd have perished of self-disgust. No relief, not even the acceptance of a common lot. I'm alive. It's impossible to repay them for this. Humanly impossible."

Peter took him by the hand:

"Bruno, you shouldn't talk like this. The only way to pay is by doing what you know you've got to do."

Bruno looked at him from behind his glasses:

"You must understand what has happened. Very few do. Great catastrophes aren't clearly visible to people who are too close. Time is needed. What has happened is that my people have been destroyed, wiped out."

In the past, Bruno would never have said anything like this. Neither in conversation nor in what he wrote did he stress his Jewish origin.

"My people don't exist any more. The Polish Jews. There were three million of them. They've perished like those here or like my parents in their Galician village. There was limitless promise, the chain of unborn generations. Great scholars, artists, writers who might have existed and now never will. Everything that was best has perished. And who was saved? A small number of those who had money. A few people like myself, assimilated, already almost Aryan. At the cost of broken solidarity."

Peter shook him by the hand.

"Don't talk like that, Bruno, Everybody alive now lives at the price of some cowardly action. I too. Everybody."

Bruno shook his head in denial.

"No, I'm guilty. Doubly guilty. What I wrote before

141

the war was empty and barren. Listening every night to jackboots echoing in the streets, I understood how empty it was. I was filled with fear: that I wouldn't have time to make up for it. No time to create something of value, to leave a trace behind. But while wanting to live, wanting time, at the same time I was destroying the value of what I might do. If my books were bad, it was because I pretended in them to be somebody I had never been."

"You'll write again and leave something of yourself to the world."

They were walking along the edge of the mounds. They saw in the distance two men digging furiously.

"They're looking for gold or maybe digging to find their dead—people killed in their rising. You say to the world: Look, over there was Naleviski Street. I should have written about it. About its daily life, about the wretched people who lived there on herrings to provide their children with an education. About the tragedy, the eternal tragedy of my people."

"You are a witness."

Bruno stopped.

"Like Josephus Flavius after the destruction of Jerusalem? Who would dare to be that? I would like to leave. I can't think here. I'm too near to everything. But they won't let me go. And I don't want to exile myself. The Polish language is my native tongue. I can't write in any other."

A large building stood alone, a fortress amidst the waves of devastation. Bruno pointed to it:

"You see, the prison was spared, it was needed. It always is. Do you remember Thaddeus? When the

Germans arrested him, he behaved bravely. He organized lectures in his cell. On what do you think?
Greek mythology. And he was taken to his death in
the middle of a story about Andromeda or Minos.
He was shot in the ruins of the ghetto. He always was
a philo-Semite."

Thaddeus, small, with a duck's nose, a black strand
of hair falling across his forehead, a satirical poet. The
one whose lines were confused by a palm-reader and
who on the thirtieth of May met death instead of love.

"All that's left for me to do," Bruno returned to
the train of his thought, "is to knock around for
awhile. Those who've been spared took new Slavic
names. Or are taking them now. To erase the past,
not to be different. But there's a feeling of shame, too.
They've given different names to a single wish to
survive. They can live on only by not being Jews.
And those who've remained Jews will emigrate."

Looking at Bruno, Peter had a feeling of guilt. A
human being's only a plaything of social forces. He
himself was one. Before the war he was apt to forget
it. There was anti-Semitism, Falangist marches, the
smashing up of Jewish shops. Did he do anything
definite? Did he oppose it openly enough? No, of
course not. And yet he was not a man of ill will;
or so he had thought. Had he the right to doubt that
theory which claims that the mysterious influences of
environment imperceptibly corrupt?

"Perhaps it's better for those who've survived to be
like Julian Halpern," he said.

Bruno was swaying as he walked, his hands clasped
behind his back.

"Better? Perhaps. The Jewish question was just an aspect of the fight against fascism. People will write and speak about the Jews as the victims of fascism—as fighters. But it's not the whole truth. A moment will come when those who try to resuscitate their memory will collide with anger. If they are kept alive in memory as they really were, it will be a bad thing. It will be called Jewish nationalism. A deviation. I'm going to try, all the same."

Peter lit a cigarette, shielding the flame with his hands.

"All this is more than I can bear."

"You've changed," Bruno smiled. "We've all changed. But if I know you at all things won't be easy for you. Here, in this country, everybody's infected by some kind of contempt for himself. You ought to go away. For a time at least."

Was there something septic in the air, or was it the panic that always accompanied the advance of this force from the East, a collective panic to which individuals succumbed by the law of social osmosis, and which was induced in him by what Bruno had said?

"Do you know, Bruno, the world outside has stopped being real for us."

"There are the Alps somewhere." Bruno was looking at the clouds over the desert of the ghetto as if he saw mountain ranges there. "I have lived within four walls, torturing myself with my thoughts, going out only rarely, because my appearance was 'uncertain.' There are limpid lakes somewhere—a great, open land."

For a long time Peter had cherished the words: to

forget. To forget the stench of prison and all that he had seen in the East: to forget Warsaw, to forget the ghetto. But could one forget? In Russia, above the curses of the guards, above the barbed wire of the camp, above the miserable wretches fighting for a bone or a piece of moldy bread, there towered in pure blue and pink the Ural mountains. A great open land.

"You may be able to manage it," said Bruno. "They're beginning already to look for people to work abroad. And they can't find them. None of the old intelligentsia is of any use. Try to have a word with Baruga."

High above, an airplane flashed in the sun, flying west. Bruno stood dark and thin, with his head thrown back, against the backdrop of ruins.

"Berlin is about to fall," he said as if reading it from the sky. "History is being made. But who knows whether the course of future events would not have been changed if some people who will never exist had been given the chance to be born."

5

FROM THE WOODS and thickets on either side of the road came the desperate mooing of cows. Their udders swollen with milk, they roamed seeking their masters, but there were no people anywhere. The white houses of the German farmers stood empty, their courtyards strewn with the down from ripped-up feather beds.

The armies were marching westward. Soviet troops

swayed along in the light, penetrating drizzle. Others, rolled in their blankets, dozed astride the barrels of guns or lay huddled together in trucks marked with American stars. They looked with apathy at the mass of humanity moving in the opposite direction. There were long rows of small carts, their horses harnessed Russian style, inching along, step by step. On the carts were piled beds, mattresses, radios, basins, sewing machines; perched on top sat women wrapped in shawls; usually the reins were held by old bewhiskered men. Deported to Germany for forced labor, these people were now returning east, a thousand, two thousand, or three thousand kilometers away, to the banks of the Don and the Volga, carrying with them what they had been able to snatch up. There were weeks or months of traveling ahead of them.

Herds of cattle moved wearily, treading heavily on their torn hooves. They were driven by Russian peasants in quilted trousers and puttees, wearing forage caps, their shoulders covered with blankets or military capes. Sometimes they would add to their herds abandoned cows that had strayed near the road. The soldiers moving west shouted envious remarks at soldiers going the other way on trucks loaded with plunder. Metal pipes, parts of boilers, coils of cable, dynamos, lathes—everything that could be removed from the factories that had escaped destruction—lay under assorted piles of household articles taken from German homes.

Those on foot moved along in small knots. They wore striped prison garb, old torn uniforms of various armies, civilian suits too large or too small for them.

146

They were grouped around pushcarts loaded with suit-cases and bundles. On some of these carts, nailed to broomsticks, were rain-soaked, clumsily sewn French, Hungarian, or Italian flags. Jews like specters clip-clopped in prison clogs or old, badly fitting boots; their peaked shaven heads on their skinny necks were only rarely covered with prison caps. Impervious to the weather they plodded on, their one aim to get as far away as possible from the places of torture from which they had been freed by the sudden collapse of the German front. But there were no women: they didn't dare show themselves on the roads on foot.

Polish ex-prisoners kept together, maintaining some-thing like order and discipline. This gave them a cer-tain feeling of security. Most of them wore prewar uniforms, patched and darned. These were the men who had been in captivity since 1939. Soldiers of the Home Army, captured in Warsaw after the failure of the rising, could be distinguished from the others by their civilian overcoats. They had been deported to camps all over the Reich; a considerable number had found themselves in that part of Eastern Germany which had now been overrun by the Red Army. The ex-prisoners marched along grimly, each with the feeling that his thoughts were following a closed circle. Ahead of them was their country and the hope of being reunited with their families. But at the same time, passing the innumerable columns of Soviet troops, they realized that they were returning to an area where military force ruled. They were bewil-dered by trying to guess what awaited them. They had already heard the news of the arrests at home. While the fighting had raged around them the possibility of escape still existed. But things had happened too quickly. They didn't know if their friends who had set off towards the West in the last days of the German *débâcle* had reached the American lines.

Stephen Cisovski, known as "Seal," had blisters on his feet. A blister always began with a hole in one's sock and an over-sized shoe; then the pain would increase until it filled one's whole consciousness and each mile to be covered became a test of will power. For Seal this problem now overshadowed everything, and the necessity of keeping on the move made him indifferent, for the first time in many months, to the conversations he overheard. These centered around the uncertain future—although cautiousness and fear that those one had trusted might prove to be dangerous were already beginning to seal lips. There were conversations about wives and mothers, about impatience and expectation. Seal did not expect anything at all. Any hope whatever seemed to him at variance with the very principle of a world which maliciously thwarts the desires of individuals. When he was a small boy, he often used to stop in front of a pastry shop and, with his nose flattened against the windowpane, dream of the taste of the unattainable cakes. He was afraid to ask his father for money to buy them. His father would have read him a lecture on the way the child of a proletarian streetcar conductor ought to behave, and tell him that the money was needed for his younger brother and sister. Later on, when he was earning his own living, or during the war years, when he was studying at an underground university, he was able to buy all the cakes he wanted. But everything always came too late, when it was no longer valuable. Now the war was drawing to a close and there was nothing ahead of him. Were his brother and sister still alive? They had been carried off at the beginning of the war to the Russian zone and now they might be anywhere—Russia, England, the Middle East.

Warsaw had ceased to exist. Catherine was no more. And yet he had had a strong faith—and this was a fault, a crime against the principle of the world. He had tried hard but in vain to reach her. Yet it had seemed to him that fate would only pursue him, never Catherine, that she would be alive and waiting. In this way he had been able almost to get rid of his anxiety about her. When he had emerged from the sewer and lay on the flagstones in the center of Warsaw, he seemed to find confirmation of his faith. Never in his life had he realized so vividly the incredible beauty of an ordinary city. Green trees; girls walking arm in arm with Home Army officers; a street radio relaying songs and communiqués. It had seemed to him as if a nightmare were over and that he would never be haunted again. Joanna, Bertrand, and Gdula were growing indistinct, melting away, becoming obliterated by the picture of a happy life. Only when he approached the house where they had lived with Catherine's mother had he felt afraid. On the first landing he had sat down and had tried to quiet his beating heart. He had rung the bell, and when he saw the face of Catherine's mother he understood.

Within a few weeks the same fate befell the center of Warsaw that had already overtaken the Old City.

The cities of men are not durable. Nothing that clings to the earth is durable. He had fought, and apparently he had fought bravely. With the usual perversity of fate, he had not been killed. In camp he had had ample time for torturing himself as much as he wished. In order to make his feeling of guilt complete, he connected his wife's death with the night he had spent with Joanna. He was amazed at himself for not having thought of it before: that by his adultery he had brought on himself the punishment of fate. He compared dates. No. Catherine was killed while moving wounded the day before the incident with Joanna. But perhaps it was the intention that counted, the readiness to break faith. And yet at the time—why? —he did not feel that he was doing wrong, no scruple of conscience had manifested itself, not even in his body. He had betrayed Catherine, he had betrayed Joanna by letting her leave the house—but could he have stopped her?—and he had betrayed Gdula, leaving him behind to die. In camp everybody kept away from him. They themselves were in a similar frame of mind—their words were edged with bitterness and pain, they quarreled and argued frequently. Usually he kept silent, but when he spoke his sarcasm was savage and accurate. Once, when he had said something about Poland and the rising, the man next to him had slapped his face. The matter had then become a question of honor and there were long, tedious complications before it was settled.

The road led through a region of hills and lakes full of glacial boulders. In the evenings they turned off the main road and spent nights in deserted farmhouses; here and there they would come across frightened families, eager to show them that they had nothing left, that everything had been taken away. The young girls were exhausted and indifferent, ready to lie with a man at the slightest gesture. They should have derived some satisfaction from this sudden humility on the part of the *Herrenvolk*. But there was no taste of victory in it; it was not as they had imagined it while prisoners. Already they were beginning to feel something near to pity—though nobody yet admitted it openly. They roasted meat over open fires and later posted sentries armed with sticks—the only weapons they had.

At the outskirts of every small town through which they passed they were met by a smell of burning: the center of each town was always completely gutted. Around the red walls of the inevitable Gothic church in the market square only the skeletons of houses and metal shop-signs twisted by the heat remained. They tried to explain to themselves this pattern of destruction. Some thought it was the result of a deliberate plan; others, that the Germans had chosen to defend the center of each town or village.

They were approaching the old Polish frontier. The local people they met were bilingual. The ex-prisoners divided themselves into groups according to their different destinations. In due course they would split up and, mingling with the mass of humanity on the move, rely from then on on their wits to get them home. Trains seemed to be running again, made up of flatcars, and you could board them for the price of a bottle of vodka. Seal was leaning on a hazel stick which bent under his weight. He thought only of the pain in his feet, of the blissful moment when he would lance the festering blisters.

6

JULIAN HALPERN, LEANING against the window frame, saw a straight, characterless street below. It was an achievement to have been officially allocated a former German apartment in Lodz that wasn't in ruins. Everybody was trying to get one; Lodz was only 150 kilometers from Warsaw and these cities were the two main centers that it was better to stay close to. He was able to sleep in a clean bed again and to be master in his own home after so many years. He had found suits and pajamas in the wardrobes and even an S.A. uniform. The Germans had left in a hurry.

On the pavement below Wolin appeared. He was punctual. Julian switched off the radio and went to open the door for him. Walking on a soft carpet still gave him a childish pleasure: he could not quite get used to it. He was amused by the slippers which the German *Hausfrau—Kirche, Küche, Kinder*—had adorned with embroidery for her spouse. Wolin hung up his khaki overcoat in the hall and looked around.

"Well, everything in the best of order. A sample of their stinking taste. Even a superb landscape, I see." He pointed to a ghastly picture of a sunset.

"But I've removed the Führer's portrait," laughed Julian. "Let me make some coffee."

"Oh, I forgot. I brought something with me." Wolin went back to the hall. "Yes, do make some coffee."

He sat down in an armchair, resting a large album on his knees.

"Changes of power are very useful. Objects acquire new owners. Here at Lodz you can get anything you want. Now things are beginning to come in from Berlin. You have to admit that the Germans could make beautiful reproductions. Look."

He showed Julian a page with a drawing by Dürer.

"Look at that peasant woman's face. Life, true realism. No prettiness. And here"—he traced a line with his finger—"the solidity of the flesh here."

Julian poured out some brandy and the coffee.

"Baruga says that in a few years his printing plant will produce the best artistic publications in this part of Europe," he said. "He's already preparing an album of Korpanov's work."

Wolin raised his glass.

"Baruga. We need people like him. For the moment."

"Well," Julian did not wish to be drawn. "He's certainly energetic."

"The talents of a partisan leader are necessary only when guerrilla warfare is in progress." Wolin's tone was sharp. "He'll get into trouble with his individualism. He always wants to go one better and guess which way the party line's going to turn next."

"Today everything's improvised. Are there many like him? After all, there's only a handful of us altogether."

153

"To recognize somebody's usefulness doesn't mean forgetting the future. At the moment we're just following in the wagon tracks of the old style. And Baruga's got that style. Aristocratic megalomania."

"What's his real name?" asked Julian.

"Stein. Son of a lumber dealer. Maybe his background explains his militaristic, dictatorial poses. Compensation. He'll never free himself from it. Every day now this tendency gets stronger in him. This brandy isn't at all bad."

"The soldiers'll swap anything for vodka. I got this for two bottles of the ordinary stuff."

"Trading. Millions are in it. The last paroxysm of their damned passion." Wolin spat the words out. "To earn money, to survive. Perhaps things will change. Perhaps their good old life will return: their freedom. Small shops, investments, acquisitions and more acquisitions, warm featherbeds. We'll change it all. We'll take them in hand. Do you know what Baruga's up to now?"

Julian did not.

"A variation on a nationalistic-Catholic theme. And it so happens that he's right. It might be useful. And now he wants to make use of the chief ideologist of the right-wing action groups, Michael Kamienski. The Russians have got him in prison."

Julian whistled. Wolin looked up with interest.

"Did you know him?"

"Of course. Polish fascists, as you know, are a rather special breed. Pure, sublime, looking up into the sky, no dirty work for them. They like to arrange

154

for things to be done for them behind their backs. I've talked to Michael about philosophy. During the occupation he even suggested hiding me. His Christian duty. Only his duty did not extend to what his units were doing."

"What's he like as a person?"

"A lot of will power. An able tactician. Well read; by instinct an N.D.* He thinks along fixed lines; doesn't understand the march of history. He's hypocritical but not cynical. Naturally he took money from the big industrialists for his movement."

"If this group is formed," Wolin said with slow deliberation, "one can foresee more or less accurately what methods they will use. Before the war they said the French Catholics were degenerate because they themselves were strong. They sometimes used Thomas Aquinas as a prop, but for them Maritain was virtually a Judeo-Communist. Now it's their turn to embark on Catholic humanitarianism and personalism—in rather plaintive tones."

"They won't attract our so-called 'progressive Catholics.' Some of those are moving quite quickly toward Marxism. The others are intransigent."

"What can we do?" Wolin stroked his cheek. "The Church is powerful. But it's not this that matters. We've got to give the whole intelligentsia some ideological syrup. Soothe their lacerated consciences. At the same time, there's no harm in trying to break one of the Vatican's teeth. What we need is simply time.

* N.D. stands for National Democrat—a member of an extreme right-wing party in Poland.

On the whole, it's more profitable to gamble with people like this Michael than monkey about with the Socialists."

"All this is going to take time and may the devil take the lot of them." Julian clasped his hands behind his head and stretched his legs. "What matters are the young people. The best of them will come over to us and come quickly—from pure disgust at the stupidity of the others. Intellectually, that crowd's completely disarmed. They've nothing to offer."

"How are things at the university?"

"Chaos, and vague indications of the shape of things to come. Anyhow, for many a year I'll have to look at the stupid faces of people adjusting themselves. I don't know if you could find three Marxists among all the professors in the country. If you could, they'd be Marxists like myself—of the latest variety."

"You should work on that book of dialectics."

"I am. Now that I've got a good place to work in."

"There'll be trouble with the Socialists," Wolin said suddenly. "Collaboration with them's a necessity, but at the same time it's a contagious disease. More than one head in the Party's going to roll one day. I can definitely promise you that. Do you remember what I asked you for?"

"Oh yes, detective stories. I haven't forgotten but I can't find any yet."

Wolin was a mystery-story addict. He said there was nothing as relaxing in days like these. He was always hunting for new ones in any language available.

"I'm also looking for anything by Labiche! A delightful writer! *The Italian Straw Hat* is going to be put on the stage."

Julian tried to pour him another brandy but Wolin covered the top of the glass with his hand.

"No, everything in moderation. I believe you're friendly with Peter Kwinto? Kwinto—what sort of a name's that? Is it his real name?"

"Yes," said Julian—slightly embarrassed, since he wondered why Wolin wanted this information. "It's an Italian name. Quinto. It should be spelled 'quinto' and not in this Polonized form. He's a descendant of some of the Italian architects and courtiers who settled here once. A nice chap. Never worried much about money. A feudal origin's better than a petty bourgeois heredity."

Wolin closed his eyes. Feudal origin. People usually assumed that he himself came from a working-class family. Yet, in fact, his childhood had been spent in a large white house in a park by a lake. His French governesses had forbidden him to splash in the water when he was taken for a walk along the graveled paths. Later he had learned how to escape, took a boat and disappeared for days on end. He was already oppressed by the unreality of his life. Real life was outside, with the village boys. The unreality became even more apparent to him when he was sent every morning in a carriage to school in a town six kilometers away. When he was fifteen he ran away from home. Since then he had been a rolling stone. Naked poverty, manual labor, the acquisition of class consciousness, the first prison sentence—he owed a lot, intellectually, to prison. Then came France, Spain, France again, Russia.

"Those who have joined forces with us have been very lucky," he said. "On the opposite side there will be a gnashing of teeth and, with every year, with every month, increasing despair. As they lose ground they won't know what's happening to them. It will be almost a physical phenomenon. You should write an analysis of a reactionary who is losing ground. It would be very interesting. What did this Kwinto write before the war?"

Julian pondered. Wolin probably knew Peter's history.

"He studied Paul Valéry. You know where that leads. He was a typical product of those literary circles of ours. Suspended in a vacuum."

"The articles he writes are quite good. Incidentally, it will take time before anyone tries to analyze Paul Valéry from the Marxist point of view. Quite a problem to assess how an artist of a decaying class buys conciseness of language at the price of an escape from reality. And why this happens. The majority of them escape from reality through the disruption of language. Kwinto, I bet, has some inner difficulties."

"That would be normal. The processes of adjustment are slow for everybody today."

"Yes." Wolin was thinking of a tendency he had observed in Julian. The tendency to minimize to himself the difficulties in the way of his ambition. In terms of ideology, everybody should get what satisfies him.

158

That was what revolutions were for. And Julian has always been sure that he deserved that university chair. "Yes, that's clear. What amuses me are these women here in Lodz. Each court has its *précieuses ridicules*. Those girls are chattering already in the new language they've picked up. Do you ever see Red Mary?"

Wolin burst out laughing. Julian, instead of answering him, was imitating Red Mary entering a political meeting. He was a very good mimic.

7

MARTYNIAK WAS SITTING on the running board of an old Ford. The road was deserted, and only at infrequent intervals did Soviet trucks roll past. Karvovski, the driver, was tinkering with the engine patiently and in silence. Things had started badly. If the engine had failed fifty kilometers from Warsaw, what was going to happen later? Martyniak was angry. He had spent the night in Praga in order to start at daybreak and had been badly bitten by bedbugs. There were swarms of them everywhere: as though they had left the burning houses in orderly columns and concentrated in the undamaged part of the city. Besides, he could not forgive himself: it was very seldom that he forgot anything of importance, but like a fool, he'd forgotten the envelope in which he kept his Party card. He was ashamed to admit it. What would his traveling companions think of him? He had all the other documents: letters of authority written in Polish and Russian. He was looking at the flat fields covered with green wheat and yawning. The early morning mist was rising and it was distinctly cool.

How quickly things were changing. Borkovski in jail; he had heard a few days ago about his arrest. And he, Martyniak, a deputy director of a factory, or at any rate going to be. He had been told quite clearly: "If you can save the paper mill and make sure that the machines aren't removed, if you can get it working —all right. If you can't—well, it can't be helped." But there was a chance all the same. These Communists weren't so bad, really. You at least knew where you were with them. You were told exactly what to do, given concrete jobs. He ought to feel grateful to Theophile for having advised him to join the Party. "Nowadays, my friend, you can't do anything without it," Theophile had said. "If you're smart you'll join now. Only the stupid are going with the Socialists. The country's going Communist anyhow. The Socialists bamboozled us long enough and they won't do it again. What does it matter to working people like us, anyhow? Things were bad and they can't get any worse, they can only get better." And he went on to analyze the situation: "The Russians are the end: complete barbarians. All they do is steal, smash, wreck things. But we've got to show them that they can't have it all their own way. The factories are ours, the railways are ours; and once there are enough of us in the Party, we'll have the whip hand. The Party Secretary's one of us. He talks sense."

Martyniak had read the Secretary's speeches and found there answers to questions which had tortured

160

him during the war years and even before that. But at that time he had not been attracted to the Communists. They shouted a lot, and the only thing that was obvious was that they were pro-Russian. Now it all looked rather different. And he liked the Secretary who had signed his credentials personally. Had it ever been possible in the old days for a great dignitary to be a simple man without any condescension toward his subordinates? Baruga, on the other hand, was rather a freak. But even he was a damn sight better than Borkovski and fools like that.

He had discussed with Theophile at length whether to set out in the questionnaire what he had done during the occupation. It was all very complicated. That underground activity of his had been inspired by London and their paper was a coalition organ. Theophile thought that he shouldn't conceal anything. "If you don't admit it, they'll find out sooner or later. Just say openly: I wasn't anybody important—just a printer. I took orders. The paper was against the Germans so I worked for it. Nobody's a saint, everybody belonged to some group or other. If they want to be choosy, they won't find anybody 'pure.' " Martyniak acted according to Theophile's advice and it did not do him any harm. But the fact that they knew about his past was far from pleasant. Perhaps one day they would dig it up? You never knew in advance. There hadn't been any point in living in fear, in hiding out from the Gestapo, if it only left a dangerous mark on your record.

Repko jogged him with the door of the car and stuck out his head.

"Well, what news?"

Karvovski looked up over the hood. He pushed his hat back and wiped his forehead with his sleeve.

"It's an old can. You can't do much with a car like this. I'm trying my best. It's got to start."

Repko got out to stretch himself. His round face with its upturned nose was puffy from lack of sleep. He was wearing a leather jacket he had bought from an airman; it was a good jacket and Martyniak admired it. The coat he had picked up somewhere was not warm enough for this time of year. Repko was a comrade from the Party. Lately he had been meeting him often and they had become friendly. By trade, he was a worker in a razor-blade factory.

"Where's the engineer?" asked Repko.

"He went to the village to buy something. He says we've got to collect food. Things'll be pretty scarce where we're going."

"Scarce or not, there'll be plenty of time to worry about it. I'm hungry."

He produced a parcel wrapped in a newspaper, and with his pocketknife divided a sausage into three parts. They ate sitting in the ditch.

Karvovski smacked his lips.

"Nice bread."

"My wife bakes it herself," Repko said.

"The Soviet soldiers say that as soon as you get to white bread and sausage, you're in Poland." Karvovski spoke with his mouth full.

A military truck passed at high speed. Repko spat.

"Those bastards haven't got anything. Even if they haven't any food, at any rate they should have some machines. But no, they want ours."

162

Martyniak was deep in thought.

"If we go on sitting here we'll never get there. The factory'll be complete all right, but it'll be in Moscow."

Karvovski laughed:

"Oh no, we'll make it somehow. God! The junk that's called a car nowadays. Look at this Ford!"

"Will we be able to get a work crew?" asked Repko. "They say it's deserted over there. But we've got to do it somehow even if it isn't easy."

Martyniak produced his cigarettes.

"We'll get a crew all right." He felt it his duty to calm his companion's fears. "It's true there aren't many people there; and those who are there are only interested in looting. But people on the way back from Germany come through there. We can appeal to their common sense. The mill will be started and they'll have work and food. Housing's no problem there. All over the place they can pinch whatever they want."

Repko didn't agree.

"A man returning from Germany wants to see his family as soon as possible. He doesn't think about what's coming next. And who believes this territory's going to stay Polish? Does anyone trust the Russians? Today they say one thing, tomorrow they might say something else. The land's German. It won't be easy."

Karvovski waved his hand: "Poland? Is this country Poland now?"

He started to tinker with the engine again. Martyniak knew he shouldn't allow these men to brood too much. But who was he to preach to his own kind?

"This is the way I see it, Repko. We've survived the Germans and we must try to get by now. Thinking won't help. Action is what matters. Doesn't everybody try to get by? Of course they do. Where are you best off? In a factory. Even if there's no money at first, things are more friendly. There'll be a plant canteen, special rations. And if there are any roundups or deportations, the factory protects you. People know all that. Anybody who's been in Russia will tell you to get into factory if you can."

The sun showed palely through the mist. Repko unbuttoned his leather jacket and stroked its flannel lining.

"True enough. Only it's a little early yet. Everybody's rushing about trying to make some money. As for myself, I've had enough of that, it's a dog's life. All through the war nothing but trading and smuggling; if you didn't you died. And now we've only got what my wife makes by trading. A man should live like a human being. I ought to enroll in a course or something. I know I'm stupid."

"Now's the time. Whoever starts now can advance quickly," said Martyniak. "There's enough room for everybody."

"Yes, of course. That's what I'm thinking too. Over there we might lay our hands on an apartment. What do you think? There'll be a lot of valuables left by the Germans. The Wild West. I'll look around. But things won't be quiet for a long time. You could easily ruin your wife and family there."

Martyniak thought that he himself ought to get married. If he hadn't been a widower before the war, would he ever have got mixed up in that underground stuff? Now he ought to settle down.

The engine started. Karvovski shouted triumphantly: "See what it means to look after your own machine! She changes her mind at once! And now if we've got to wait for the engineer, don't blame me."

"Here he is," said Martyniak. A few hundred yards from where they were sitting Wolski appeared in knickers and ski-boots on the road between the houses of the village. A rucksack was on his back.

"Before the war he wouldn't have been a director. Much too young," remarked Repko.

"They say he's a real expert. There aren't many of them. People like that don't have to join the Party."

"The intelligentsia. They had the money to study. I'm going to send my children to school, no matter what happens. Without a trade you're nobody."

"He won't be in the way, he'll have his boiler room. And the rest is our responsibility. If we keep together we'll do all right."

Repko pulled his cap down and got up.

"I don't know a damn thing about paper. Well, we'll see."

Karvovski was at the wheel. He was blowing the horn and shouting to Wolski.

"Our limousine's working again. Let's get going."

8

"SOON MY MOMENT will come," Peter said to himself as he steered the conversation toward the problem of Polish workers in France. Baruga, his shirt unbuttoned, was scratching his hairy chest. Peter suddenly remembered the school desks and the grooves he had carved in them with his pocketknife. For many years he had been an indifferent pupil at school and had got bad marks for conduct. Try as he would, nothing came out right until one day he had understood what school meant and what was required from him. The reason for his failure was simple: he had tried to say what he thought and, what was worse, in his essays he had been ashamed to use sentences which had no connection with his personal and often very unformed views. There were endless troubles over this; the other boys, even the stupidest ones, learnt the knack long before he did. As a result, he had rebelled against his surroundings and, out of simple naïvete, behaved like a wild anarchist. The teachers did not ask for an impossible sincerity. Their task was to create a social ritual and to adjust the young to it.

When Peter wrote two pages of a literary essay in order to please his teacher everything changed suddenly. He had never forgotten his amazement at the time. His pen moved smoothly over the paper; he allowed himself to be guided by the logic of a reasoning that was independent of truth and falsehood; it had its own validity. And what was more important, when he tried to control himself, nothing intelligent came into his head. He suffered from a lack of ideas and earned comments like: "Subject undeveloped. Style too concise, too telegraphic." But later, ideas rushed to him of their own accord and he caught them with the greatest ease. He received a good grade, and when he applied this method to his whole behavior at school, he soon became one of the best students in

166

his class. The whole secret lay in a pliant yielding to social pressure; it was important not to believe too much in what was recommended (which would be bad, for it would have cramped him internally), and not to believe too little. And what else had he been doing since his release from camp? He was falling back into his old school habit—though it was only at this moment that he had realized it, while talking to Baruga. The new system was just like a big school, and millions of people had discovered its mechanism. It was not in the least important to accept it with sincerity; but when expressing an opinion, it was necessary to make internal arrangements to insure that you really believed what you were saying. Five minutes later you could begin to doubt privately (as in school in front of the blackboard) every single word.

If he were to play a Machiavellian comedy in front of Baruga, it would obviously be a mistake. Peter's thoughts worked in harmony with his words but his internal control system was alert to prevent any deviations from the course.

"I'm interested in France," he said. "I can't imagine what it will look like after the war. I'm not the same person. I'd see things there I'd never seen before. When we begin to get organized there, I hope you'll remember me. I could be useful. Six months in France are just what I need."

Baruga yawned. Another one. But the fact that people were coming to him, that it would soon be in his power to move people about like pawns on a chessboard, here and all over Europe—perhaps even in

Asia, Africa, and America—was very agreeable. Well, like everybody else, the boy had a bad dose of Westernitis. Whether he wanted to escape or not was of no importance. He had been hit too hard for it not to have left deep traces. Anyone who had tasted that bitter draught walked around looking normal—but with everything turned upside down inside. Give him ruins, fear, misery, and he would long for little gardens, houses with green shutters, peace. Give him *Gemütlichkeit* and he would moan and wriggle; a small part of him was missing, something which once made all that acceptable to him. And he would be choked by the senselessness of life. That's where we catch them. When they begin to recognize the nonsense of life, they're ours. Then they have to act—at any price. And who but we can give them the moment of delight, of enchantment, the sense that they are demigods?

"You speak French fluently, of course."

"In some ways I should look on a job like this simply as a kind of cure. You understand, don't you, that during all those years a lot of claustrophobia got bottled up inside. I feel a sort of desperate hunger for a change of scene, for a different rhythm of life. But perhaps we ought to put all this off until you see the suitable opportunity."

Baruga prided himself on knowing instinctively the best psychological approach to an individual. To each his own; only that way could you attract people and make them give you loyal service. What about this Kwinto? Undoubtedly very ambitious. And one of the gentry. He had a so-called "decency," a certain

168

generosity of manner. What if one loosened the chains and took a chance on this ambition and decency? The best chains were invisible. After all, he came to me with his problem. To escape, simply to desert—that would be perfectly simple in the middle of all this chaos. But no, Kwinto wouldn't do that.

He said gently:

"It seems to me, Kwinto, that you ought to get some fresh air into your lungs. You ought to see the world. You've got the eye of a journalist, the talent of a born reporter. It shouldn't be wasted. I'd be rather inclined to make you our foreign correspondent. We'll think about it when we've sorted some of this mess out."

A confused vision of a break with everything, of an indefinable freedom, came into Peter's mind. The old dream about the end of school. He suppressed it immediately. To have this vision simply meant lying to Baruga and therefore unmasking himself. And when he was two-faced toward Baruga was he not in fact two-faced toward himself? If he had at moments the intention of escaping, he only played with it, didn't quite believe it was real. What was there for him in the wide world? A return to his own past self? Impossible and repulsive. It was conceivable that after the amnesty he might have left with the Polish Army for Persia. But it happened otherwise. Could one become an *émigré* today, knowing it was forever, acquiescing completely in eternal defeat? It would mean plunging into a bottomless void; there was nothing to hold on to; it was beyond comprehension; it would be a futile denial of the failure of the old guard, who today were fading so fast from the world of reality. Each gesture, each thought, each decision of theirs was infected with failure, just as that dreadful rising had been. His cunning was only make-believe. He wasn't really pretending to Baruga at all.

If there was any guile in his mind it arose from sources deeper than thought: it was the instinctive knowledge of a watchful organism. Tread softly. Gain time. He was too weak—still too weak—to jump. An animal measures in one glance the breadth of the ravine and knows whether its muscles will carry it to the other side. If the ravine is too wide it looks for a way down the slope.

Baruga, at his most cordial, was sitting in front of him like a confessor. When he was at school, Peter had met one of those catchers of souls. Quite unlike their severe and fanatical chaplain, he would take the hand of a young rebel into both of his, and look warmly and compellingly into his eyes. It was disarming; but at the same time Peter had suspected the priest of being a hypocrite, and what is worse, hypocritical toward himself. Baruga too, it seemed to him, was never entirely natural. All his poses—a catcher of souls, a patron, a Maecenas—were artificial. All, with the exception of those outbursts of terrible anger —but even those would come to an end too abruptly. Perhaps Baruga used them too as a means to an end. What was real in him? Belief in the doctrine? Certainly not its official side; Baruga had been in Russia. Faith in historical necessity as an instrument of his will? Peter would have given a lot to be able to talk to Baruga with complete frankness, but it was impossible. Every word Baruga uttered had a tactical aim.

And when alone, did he continue to think only in terms of tactics? When human beings become part of a system, maybe they cease to have a center, a core, any personality entirely real and their own. Perhaps they really become the figures whose role they have learned to play. And what if one were to judge Baruga by absolute standards of truth and untruth? One would revert to the anarchism of adolescence. One would have to spit in his face.

"The secret of style" said Baruga, "is to understand history."

"It depends on you," that young man had said. Baruga did not like these evenings—very rare, for that matter—when a gap intervened between the chaos of the day and the conferences he held at night. He was haunted then by an obsession with old age and death. He was being swept round and round in a whirlpool and all the while looking for confirmation of the fact that he was really playing a vital part. At one time he had dreamed of preserving himself forever through some immortal work of art. But he had learned since that nothing of the kind existed. Bubbles on the wave of history. And when he was manipulating the creators of supposedly immortal works, tasting their flattery and observing their cowardice, he could only laugh at the naïve illusions that ascribed some imperishable gifts to man. A man can be great only through the art of action, the art of using his fellow-men. But even this didn't last. And one day, after hundreds of years, when everything had been ground up and re-ground? He got up.

"Yes, yes. You must go on working. I want you to

171

write about the plans for the reconstruction of Warsaw. Everybody's going to be enthusiastic about that. The rebuilding of Warsaw will unify the divided nation."

9

THE VILLAGES WERE drenched with warm spring rain. They were full of whispers, rumors, frightening and contradictory news. Decrees invalidating from day to day the banknotes in circulation had increased the peasants' distrust of the currency. They clung to gold coins and dollars and waited for a change. Everything was uncertain. People said that nothing mattered because another war would break out soon; or that a new government would take over, not the Russian-sponsored one; but no one could tell how. There was a general feeling that things could not go on as they were. It was not easy to discover who was strong in the world and who was afraid. The officers of the armies passing through to the West boasted that they were going far, to France, to the shores of the Atlantic: "Europe is ours." Some neighbor would tell what he had heard from the priest about the sixteen-member underground government. When the Russians had entered the country these men had been hiding near Warsaw. A Russian general had guaranteed their safety with his word of honor if they would come into the open and meet with him. When they arrived at the appointed place they were arrested and deported to Russia. The landlords' estates were

172

being divided among the peasants hurriedly, haphazardly, without rhyme or reason. Some people assumed from this that the new government was afraid, but others said that the distribution of land was a joke and that they were going to take the land back and organize collective farms.

There was a shortage of horses, cattle, and pigs—much stock had been destroyed by the soldiers passing through. Strange, unknown diseases were spreading. Young men were afraid to touch girls; the doctor in the nearest town had issued warnings about Asiatic syphilis. Some of those who had been deported to Germany were coming back. They told about the territories in the West, about great areas lying fallow waiting to be appropriated. Some of the poorer peasants were already considering whether to leave their meager plots of ground and move there in search of happiness. The most important thing was never to reveal one's thoughts. The peasants had learned during the German occupation that a person who wished to survive must know how to keep silent. They had made a strict habit of silence in those years; nothing must be mentioned of what had happened in the village at night or who had passed through it—partisans, Jews, or escaped prisoners of war. Now, as then, living was dangerous. Though the young men had hidden their arms and pretended they had never taken part in anything, many had been arrested by the Russians on the word of informers. Here and there the Polish secret police would appear suddenly, carry out a search, and shoot a few people; they were worse than the Gestapo. The old women crossed themselves in awe—everything since the beginning of the war was a fulfillment of the prophesies about the rule of the Antichrist.

Kord's detachment was keeping away from the towns. It was some thirty strong. Its commander, a stocky man, an alert machine of agile muscles, had been wounded in the 1939 campaign, had escaped being captured, recovered from his wounds, and for some years roamed the forests. With varying success he had fought battles against the Germans, attacking their storage dumps and transports. When the Russians entered the country, he did not surrender his arms to them as ordered by his superiors. This proved to have been wise. Those who surrendered to the Russians were received with politeness and honored as allies in the fight against Hitler. But a little later they were herded behind barbed wire and finally deported to the East. Kord's unit had avoided that fate but their situation was desperate. They were waiting for instructions from London and no instructions arrived. Most of the young soldiers had drifted away to begin life again as civilians. But new men, for whom the secret police was searching, kept joining the unit.

Kord went into town once, trying to establish contact with a network of conspirators that was fast breaking up, and was nearly caught. The new method, never used with such precision by the Gestapo, was called "the kettle." It conformed to the Russian passion for discretion and for the settlement of everything without fuss: terror was becoming something mysterious and indefinable, looming larger and more ghastly because of the uncertainty as to where and how it would strike. "The kettle" was worked by the police—the NKVD

174

or the Polish secret police—laying an ambush in one's apartment or house. Everybody who rang the bell—whether a peddler or a man from the electricity company—was politely invited in, and kept there. The police would wait a week, even two or three, until several people had been caught. Everybody detained was supplied with food and examined on the spot. Kord made light of stories about "kettles." However, when he was actually in the doorway of a house where he knew a very important unit of the underground press was located, he suddenly decided to send his lieutenant in first.

As things were, the new authorities were concentrated mainly in the towns. They would make armed expeditions into the countryside, but there, those who knew the terrain were at an advantage. Kord could count everywhere on help from the peasants. They would warn him, show him danger points, and many of them would join in his operations; afterward they would hide their arms in trees and return to work.

What future was there in it? Neither Kord nor any of his men could find an answer. It was better to live like this than in prison. They could hope that there was some truth in the rumors about a new war: the Western allies could not be so stupid now, while their armies were still mobilized, as to allow the Russians to overrun so many lands. Diplomatic talks were, of course, only a temporary expedient. As for the new coalition government which included some of the London politicians, Kord thought that any politician willing to talk with the Bolsheviks was a villain: the Russians' failure to help the Warsaw rising, their arrest

175

of the Home Army men, the trap they set for the sixteen members of the underground government—such
acts meant one thing only, even for those who wanted
to forget the pact with Hitler, the year 1939, Katyn,
and the hundreds of thousands deported to labor
camps. Occupation by a foreign power was a fact and
one had to act accordingly. Traitors should be pun-
ished. The people in general must be made to realize
that collaboration with the occupying forces—as formerly collaboration with the Germans—was punish-
able by death. Only this one means of resistance
remained: to prevent the group of agents established
in Warsaw by Moscow from enrolling supporters
attracted by the desire to safeguard their own skins or
by the prospect of future benefits.

One of the most trusted soldiers in Kord's gang was
Gdula. How he had avoided death in Warsaw, he did
not know. He remembered only the frightful moment
when he saw a grenade come through the window.
When he came to, the white coif of a nun was all he
could see. From the story told by the Sisters he tried
to reconstruct what had happened. He was brought
to the hospital by a German doctor, who had said:
"This young bandit's the only one left alive at this
barricade," and instructed the nuns to report at once
to the authorities if he began to get better. "He was a
strange German," the Sisters told him, "he spoke in
French and his accent wasn't German. He asked what
medicines we needed and brought them to us the next
day." A few months later Gdula went back to his little
home town where his father was a minor official in
the local government. That had been a wonderful
period. Stuffed with delicacies by his mother, basking

in the glamor of having been a defender of the Old City, he enjoyed comparative peace and even became a sort of local hero. This popularity was not altogether fortunate. About two weeks after the entry of the Russians—at the beginning of February—the house of his family was surrounded and Gdula was sure that he was on his way to Siberia; but he succeeded in escaping through the orchards. From then on there was only the forest left. Kord, who was operating in the vicinity, accepted him willingly. Adaptation to the new kind of life was difficult at first. They travelled by rapid marches, spending the nights, whenever the villages seemed unsafe, on beds of pine needles. But soon things began to get easier, and because of his cheerfulness and his jokes, he got on well with the others. Kord took a liking to him and discovered he had a first-rate talent for foraging. Gdula, too, liked his commander: he was energetic, strict, and never had moments of hesitation, making all decisions on the spur of the moment. He was guided not by reasoning but by a sixth sense developed during years of partisan warfare.

The forests were crisscrossed with trenches and foxholes. In the autumn of 1944, the Germans had built a whole system of fortifications which they never used—the Soviet tanks kept turning their flanks and they had had to retreat in a hurry. Just as after the 1939 campaign, a lot of equipment left was lying around. In thickets, partisans sometimes found rusting rifles beside the corpses of German soldiers. Once, at night, lying on the slope of a wooded hill, they heard quite close by a noise like someone smacking his lips; it came from the direction of some concrete

bunkers. Kord forbade his men to go near. He took
Gdula and a few others, and before dawn they crawled
silently to the bunkers and lay in wait. They pounced
on a man who came out, and pinned him to the
ground. He was a terribly thin, bearded, dirty German, shaking with fright. What could be done with
him? Kord questioned him thoroughly. He turned out
to be a Wehrmacht soldier, not an S.S. man. He had
been living on frozen potatoes which he dug up from
the fields. When he realized who they were, he begged
them to let him join them. Kord said no.

"I don't need a Boche to help me. Whether he lives
or dies is no business of mine."

When they moved on, they gave the German a slab
of bacon.

10

IT WAS THE worst time of day for driving. Karvovski switched on the headlights but their wavering
beams melted into the uncertain twilight. Since leaving
Warsaw they had covered only two hundred kilometers.
The engine was not giving them half so much trouble
now as the tires; with one patch on top of another,
they repeatedly went flat and everybody began to bet
on which was going to go next. They began to think
about finding beds for the night and decided to stop
at the next village. The road was empty: it ran
straight, like a ribbon stretched between the heather
and the pine forests. Martyniak was sitting in front;
he remarked to Karvovski that he might see better

with the lights switched off. The driver tried that. Far in front they could see the sunset sky over the jagged treetops. The wheels kept jolting into holes in the road made by the caterpillar tracks of tanks.

"Can't see a thing," said Karvovski, switching on the lights again.

Martyniak had suggested switching off the lights because he felt uneasy. In this deserted area it would be better not to announce one's presence too much in advance. You never could tell what might happen. Repko was yawning in the back seat. "I'm shaken to pieces. And there's not even room to stretch yourself."

Marshes appeared with a grayish-yellow expanse of dry reeds. Here and there shone slivers of water, like long narrow blades. Wild ducks were rising. Further on, they were suddenly surrounded by dark forest, by tall ancient trees. Wolski lit a match and looked at his watch:

"If nothing goes wrong we should be there in half an hour."

Karvovski braked violently and Martyniak hit his forehead against the windshield. "What the hell?" he exclaimed. At the same time, he saw a pair of legs in high boots in the middle of the road. When you're afraid that something's going to happen, it hardly ever does. But it has this time, he thought. He had a superstition that things like that could be averted simply by half-expecting them.

Things were happening exactly as in a gangster film. Cold metal was pressed against his neck: "Get out!" "Put your hands up!" The headlights were switched off. They were surrounded by shadowy figures in

179

peasant's jackets or short sheepskins, armed with automatic pistols. "Chicago stuff!" said Repko. Wolski burst out laughing. "I'll teach you to laugh!" a voice yelled. "Search them! Take everything they've got in their pockets!" The barrel of a pistol was stuck against Martyniak's shoulder blade. Strange hands went over his body. "Hands behind your heads! March!" They started into the dusk along the sandy road. Martyniak kept stumbling against roots. The engine was started again, tree trunks appeared in the light, and he saw in front of him the clasped hands of Karvovski and the ski-cap of the man who was following him. The road was winding now and the car which was following slowly behind lit it for short moments only, making it more difficult to walk in the darkness when the road twisted. Jump to the side? Useless. The hard object kept knocking against his back as he moved. When a man really wants something, everything goes wrong. Whatever he decides, things never turn out right. He felt a sudden surge of self-pity. In this new system, in Communism, there was something horrible —he knew it, yet pretended not to know. Under one set of words was hidden another, the eyes and faces of the men from the Party expressed some secret understanding and a threat: just wait and see. He had escaped from the old setup because there was nothing in that, no support, no latent strength. You wait and see. Now he saw. Everybody loathed them. You could never admit to anyone that you belonged; shame closed your mouth; and if you chose to join them, not only did you have to keep up with them but you became separated immediately from the crowd in the trains, in the streets, in the streetcars. In the old days, during the war, he had always been part of everything, one among many in a crowd. Now it was all coming to an end. There would be no factory, no new life. And what if he tried to escape? He decided to wait for a suitable moment. What if he suddenly crouched down? Only one step. But now the headlights were spotlighting the undergrowth and they were entering a clearing.

Heads were bent over a small flame on the ground. Pine needles crackled as they burned and then branches were thrown on. The four men stood in a row. They let their hands fall. From the other side of the firs a short man in a sheepskin jacket with a leather belt was looking at them. A revolver in its holster pulled his belt down to one side. His head was bare, his hair cut short. He had a small black mustache and his face was cut by a vertical scar across his nose. When the fire flared up it lit the eyes of many men sitting in a circle and flashed on the metal of their weapons. Then all was dark again and only their presence and their whispering remained.

Wolski began to speak: "Gentlemen . . ." The man growled: "Silence! No one asked you to speak." Karvovski stood with his head bowed. Repko kept shifting his weight from one foot to another. "Take off that Bolshevik jacket of his," the man ordered. Repko began to undo the buttons. They tore off his leather jacket and left him standing in a coat fastened high at the neck.

A young boy came out of the darkness, saluted, and handed their wallets to the commander. He went through them and read all their papers, holding them close to the flickering flames.

"Engineer Wolski, which is that? The Director," he recited and looked up. "One of those yellow bastards who run factories for the Communists and say they're doing it for Poland."

With a sweeping gesture he flung the open wallet into the fire. The leather curled up, smoking and hissing.

"John Martyniak? Employed by the People's Culture Press. Deputy director of a paper mill. Party member?"

Martyniak felt a glimmer of hope. He suddenly remembered that his Party card had been left behind and wasn't among the documents in his wallet. He said in a stifled voice:

"No."

The man stopped going through the papers and looked at Martyniak attentively—not at his face, but at his hands. Martyniak understood that some kind of judgment was being made. He repeated snatches of a prayer to himself. The man suddenly bared his white teeth in an ironical smile which Martyniak could not decipher, though he concentrated his attention like a dog trying to understand what was being asked of him. The man transferred the money to his pocket, and then threw everything else into the fire. Martyniak watched numbly as his authorization to take over the factory went up in flames.

"Karvovski, a driver? What did you do before the war?"

"I drove a taxi in Warsaw."

The man made a movement with his hand; a square of oilcloth was flung across the fire and hit Karvovski in the chest. Industriously he began to pick up the scattered bits of paper from the ground.

"Stanislas Repko. Personnel director of the paper mill at Eichenberg. A member of the Communist Party. Boys"—the man turned his head—"what do we call a Pole who joins the Bolshevik party and helps to enslave his own land?"

From the darkness a chorus of voices replied: "A traitor." The echo carried the words, returned, and there was silence again. The sparks were flying and circling. Repko rocked from side to side.

"I . . ."

"Shut up. You're a traitor to your country. You thought if you joined the Party you'd be safe, eh? But there's still some justice. We see that justice gets done."

The man's hand was resting on the butt of his pistol. Repko crossed himself once, then a second time. Under his turned-up nose his open mouth moved as if he wanted to shut it but couldn't.

The man made a sign—and before Martyniak understood that he was signaling to the people who stood behind him, Martyniak saw metal, the mouth of the barrel. His knees became weak. Death.

The echo repeated two shots. It came back once more from the distance, from the dark depth of the forest. He was alive and breathing. Not me. It was only Repko lying face downward. He was jerking, his fingers were closing on the moss. His cap had fallen into the fire and there was a smell of burning cloth.

The commander disappeared. Martyniak heard behind him: "Hands behind your heads! March!" The hard object was again prodded into his back. Darkness closed around him; he walked blindly. "Now they'll finish me off in a corner," he thought. He tried to understand the commander's smile. It seemed a knowing smile. Where were they being taken? He moved with difficulty but whenever he stopped he was given a shove with the barrel. His pants legs were soaked. Even if the man doesn't kill me himself the others will. That's what always happens. Under his feet he felt the slippery pine needles. Then swampy ground. His shoes were wet through; each step produced a gurgling sound. Slowly he grew used to the darkness and began to take heart. How long all this had lasted —one hour, two hours—he could not tell. He was wading now through sand and then he stopped. Something was missing: he didn't feel the touch of the pistol any longer. He stood unmoving. Not a sound. Only the murmur of pines. He sat down. Nothing. He got up again and took a few steps backward. He could not believe it yet. He listened. Then he called softly: "Karvovski! Wolski!" "Hello there," he heard. They began to call one another. Karvovski was breaking the branches and trying to get through to him. "God damn it to hell," he said to Martyniak breathlessly.

11

THE THOUGHT OF any normal life was disturbing. Supposing he were to discard his uniform—what next? If you've got something you want to do, that keeps you going. But when you arrive at the end of the journey and find nothing there except emptiness, chill, and hatred? Winter had found none of his relatives alive except his mother's brother, Isaac Friedmann. Friedmann before the war was a country Jew —he wore thick peasant boots and spent his time in a wagon buying feathers in the surrounding villages. Entering a small drygoods shop in the main street of Lodz one day, Winter saw his uncle behind the counter. Uncle Isaac leaned forward on his hands, his eyes began to blink, and he came out from behind the counter and looked at his nephew incredulously: "Little Joe? You, a soldier? Have you been to Russia?" For the first time since his return, Winter was moved. Visiting the ruins of the ghetto, all he had felt was reluctance to look at that symbol of the anonymous death of his parents. The two men embraced each other. Uncle Isaac's broad face was burnt red by the sun; he had no mustaches and was dressed in a town suit. "Well, what do you know," he laughed. "And I've come back from there, too! We've both been to the land of socialism!"

Friedmann with his wife and children had arrived in Lodz a month before in a train full of Polish Jews released from the U.S.S.R. Once out of the freight car in which they had traveled for several weeks packed in with a wretched mass of people like themselves, they looked around for a way of earning a living, found some premises previously occupied by Germans, and opened a shop. When Winter and his wife called on them for supper the same evening the table was laden with delicacies. Uncle Isaac stood rubbing his hands with pleasure, proud of his new wealth which—he made no attempt to deny it—had resulted from a few lightning transactions in currency, vodka, and loot from Germany. His two boys in their teens, wearing new suits, were shy and awkward; they were embarrassed by conversation conducted in an unfamiliar language; they themselves spoke a mixture of Yiddish and Russian.

Uncle Isaac asked Winter about his plans for the future. "Well, you must have got over it by now, I suppose?"

"Got over what?"

Friedmann's expression was roguish: "That communism you used to suffer from. The motherland of the proletariat's good for one's health. *Oy, oy,* how good for one's health!"

Winter answered reluctantly that if the Friedmanns and he himself were alive, it was only because they had been in Russia.

His uncle winked at him:

"What are you afraid of? We're among ourselves. I was arrested and deported. And why? To do me good? And where did they take me? To great big forests where you feel like an insect and everything you cut down grows up again in no time. We were

S.H.E. Nobody knew what it meant. After the amnesty we found out—Socially Harmful Elements. It meant a life sentence. There was a whole forest there cut down ten years before we arrived. All the timber was rotten—worm-eaten; there were no trucks to transport it. And the people who cut the trees down— S.H.E., too—had rotted there as well. Cossacks from the Kuban deported because they wouldn't join collective farms. But what had I done? Had I meddled in politics? Had I too much money? Maybe little Jews like me with one goat to their name were a threat to their order?"

Winter met the eyes of his wife. Her narrow chin rested on the collar of her military tunic, which was too wide for her neck. Since their sojourn at Ashabad and the death of their child, she had been a silent and fanatical enemy of the doctrine. Mrs. Friedmann, a fat woman with a ravaged face, was speaking in a sing-song voice:

"If it weren't for the fact that Isaac has a good head on his shoulders, we would have died of hunger there. You fulfill your norm, you get bread; you don't fulfill it and you don't get any. But if you want to fulfill your norm, the ration isn't enough. So we began to trade with the collective farms. They're so poor that they haven't enough bread for themselves. They exchanged potatoes for bread."

Friedmann clapped Winter on the shoulder and urged him to eat more.

"You've seen yourself, Joseph, the sort of country it is. If you've money you can get anything. The poor have legs swollen from hunger while the NKVD stuff themselves with wine and poultry. They're bandits, anti-Semites, robbers."

"So what are you going to do? Stay here and work for them?" he asked. "The same thing's going to happen here—though not right now maybe. This is no place for us. The Poles hate us. What else is there for us? A cemetery. Her relations," he pointed to his wife, "are in Palestine. That's our country. We're going there. But we can't go immediately. We got back here ruined and naked. We've got to earn some money, get some clothes, while trading's still allowed. In a year or two they'll shut the shops. Just like over there. All of us think the same. They'll let the Jews go. And if they don't, we'll try to get out anyway through Czechoslovakia and Vienna."

Winter was thinking of his father. If he were alive, would he, too, dream of Palestine? And would he himself part company with his father—in the name of what? He was suddenly visited by a desire to lose himself in a mass of his own kind. The dirty street in Warsaw where he had played with other children amid the din of street-trading and the shouts of Jewish porters, returned to his memory as a symbol of warmth, movement, happiness.

"Before they arrested me I met that fellow Teitelbaum who had a business next to your father's bindery. I asked him how he liked the new socialist life. He said: 'What's wrong with it? Two per cent live well!' And he clutched his head in his hands and shouted: 'But, man, how do you get into that two per cent?!' I tell you, Joseph," Friedmann lowered his voice, "it's true. No decent person will stay here.

People who want to get on will stay. They'll serve in the NKVD as informers, they'll join the Party, serve in ministries. Is that any sort of life? To be terrified all the time of being jailed for no reason at all. And what will the end be? If there's ever a change, the Poles will get their knives out and there won't be any Jews left. And why do you think they need people like you? Because they haven't any others, any Poles. When they've trained enough new Communists they'll promote anti-Semitism on the quiet. Just like over there: 'You've an aunt in Palestine? *Oy,* that's bad. The cousin of your brother-in-law lives in America? *Oy,* that's worse.' "

The look on Mrs. Winter's face was triumphant. She did not give vent to her feelings, for her training had been too thorough. Several times in the past few weeks Winter had had to reproach her bitterly for a lack of caution that could endanger them both. Her tongue was itching; she wanted to tell the world what she felt. She pestered him with questions: "What's going to happen to us? Tell me, Joseph. Think, decide something. I'm not going to bear children for you here."

Friedmann guessed Mrs. Winter's state of mind. "What more can I tell you? I'm sure your wife thinks the same. I'm not saying anything against you—if you must, you must. Swear you love them, applaud and cheer. You can go far here, your education will be useful. And in Palestine what could you expect? You would have to work in a *kibbutz* with your own hands. You would be a poor Jew, nothing more. If you choose another country there's not much future either—only selling or a factory. What advice can I give you? Everybody looks for something better. Even for a rope round his neck if that's better."

After that visit to the Friedmann's, Winter was on edge. But he went there often, clinging to this family life. He had no answer to his uncle's reasoning, but why he hadn't he didn't know. His uncle had said nothing unusual; he knew it all quite well. But to know was one thing and to hear someone actually saying it was another. So great was the power of silence about certain matters—it was the rule in the East and in the army—that it was a relief to hear certain of one's own thoughts actually formulated. Moreover, official language deprived experience of reality; Winter had seen at close range the means by which a person looking at a house could be persuaded that it was not a house but a cloud. His uncle was a simple man and it was difficult to discuss abstract questions with him. Yet in spite of this he had to recognize the value of his common sense. For who am I to walk about forever in my armor of doctrine and theory? His uncle touched, without knowing it, his most vulnerable spot: his longing for direct, uncomplicated contact with other people, for earning his living without ideological complications. How he wished that his education did not have to be of use, that he could work as a hand in a *kibbutz;* not as a foreman or any sort of boss—just as one among many.

When he caught himself thinking such things, Winter was horrified. Could events take an unforeseen and unpremeditated course? "They" would get everywhere sooner or later; it was no use trying to hide. And what would be left for him if he betrayed the Party? Where would he find sense or reason if by his decision he tried to prove that history had neither sense nor reason? He envied his uncle and people like him because they had never experienced the moment of poisonous understanding, had never tasted the apple from the tree of knowledge.

So long as he remained here, where every day he could watch the triumph of the idea to which he had given so much, his past had some justification. Even his experiences at the beginning of the war in the Russian zone, which he did not like to recall. He had been stupid then. And as if to remind him, he had later come across Kwinto himself, just when he was beginning to be ashamed and sorry for what he had done. They had called him to the NKVD and the conversation was friendly. He was glowing inwardly with a pleasant feeling that they were treating him like one of themselves, devoted to the cause, trustworthy. To hide anything from them would be a betrayal of their trust. What a stupid ass he'd been. And he'd been afraid to lie to them. When they asked him about Peter Kwinto he blurted out all he knew. The morning he heard about Peter's arrest was bitter for him. He tried to persuade himself that if he hadn't told them anything they would have found it out from somebody else. Only through the realization that he, Winter, was just one of a million beings through which a current was passing, moving them here and there against their will, could he get some peace. But he was glad that Peter had escaped unscathed. Supposing a human being must himself find the justification for his actions? What justification had he? When he thought like that he broke out in a cold sweat. And although he himself was anxious for the company of his uncle and aunt, he was angry with his wife for her sudden close friendship with the Friedmanns.

12

IMMEDIATELY BEHIND THE village the stony road, wasted by the rains, led up to the edge of the forest. Wolin was walking slowly, slapping a stalk against the leg of his boot. He had had enough for the day. Hadn't his ancestors used all sorts of riffraff to keep the peasants under control? Factotums, lackeys, overseers had hung for centuries around the gentry's door, leering and obsequious, ready to do any diry trick at a gesture. That kind of creature was the loyal executor of the orders of anybody who had power. And the dirty work was always carried out by the same type of person; it was a matter almost of biological formation. Specimens like this wouldn't be useful for more than a few years; they would be too stupid for the new standards. But on the whole, the apparatus of terror would produce the same types as in Russia. Thugs like this one, for violence; assorted hunchbacks and cripples with inferiority complexes; the children of the aristocracy, the refined ones, who would learn quickly that this was a good berth for people whose progress in other directions was barred because of their unsuitable origins.

Now he'll have to be promoted. When Wolin got out of the car he had been waiting for him, glowing with pleasure. He had a walleye; his fat face was flushed with vodka and the anticipation of praise. He had smashed up Kord's band. Wolin thought it was probably an accident, a fluke. Of course, he praised the man; but Wolin did not believe what he was told of the long and careful preparations that had been in progress when they suddenly found on a forest path the three men whom Kord had surprised while traveling on official business.

In the courtyard of the hut lay a row of long objects covered with peasants' shawls. At a sign from their walleyed chief, the security men uncovered the corpses. There were six of them. "This one is Kord himself." He pointed his body out to Wolin, who touched the tip of his boot to the face with a small mustache and a scar across the nose. The dead man was dressed only in a shirt and trousers; around his bare neck he wore a metal cross on a black ribbon; his feet in their mud-covered socks were spread wide. Wolin suddenly had the strange idea that it was someone he had known at school. He stopped and looked again—but the face was unfamiliar. "We got him by surprise," the man said. "He was running these villages pretty much as he pleased. But we got wind of him from one of our agents. He put up a fight. We lost two men." "And this one?" Wolin pointed with his boot to the corpse of an old peasant. "What was he? A partisan, too?" "No, he owned the hut. His son was with Kord but we didn't catch him. Before we leave we'll burn the hut down. It'll teach them a lesson." "Don't," said

193

Wolin. "This is enough. And remember to reward the informer."

The investigation of the prisoners began. Only three had been taken alive. Two softened up after being beaten and began to talk; the other was stubborn. Suddenly he tore himself away from the agents who were holding him, leaned across the table at which Wolin was sitting, and spat in his face. This was interesting. Wolin had wanted to tell them to leave the man alone, but before he could say anything they felled him with a blow on the head from a rifle butt. What was the name of this young firebrand? Gdula. Probably false; it would be as well to find out his real name. What spontaneous reactions! Wiping his face with a handkerchief, Wolin pondered the changes that intellectual sophistication caused in human behavior. His forebears had sought satisfaction for insults with sabres in their hands. Sanguine, violent, with fiery tempers that rose at the slightest provocation, they were a world of men set apart, leading their own insulated lives. Gdula certainly considered him a criminal. Only by assuming that individuals are in some way morally responsible can you achieve such spontaneous reactions. Not an easy thing in the twentieth century. When the masses begin to understand that nobody is personally responsible, they become apathetic; then it is easy to mold and shape them. The social machinery begins to seem inevitable and invincible, just as floods, tempests, and barren soil appear to primitive tribes. The modern system of government is impossible unless that belief is firmly planted. And the first to understand it, the man who had created a system that now spread fear in all the countries of

194

the globe was Felix Dzerzhinski, a Polish nobleman like himself. To Wolin's parents, Dzerzhinski was a renegade just as he, Wolin, was one to Gdula. Yet Dzerzhinski's monument would one day be erected in Red Warsaw. And of the rest of them, with their vulnerable honor, only ashes would remain.

The road, the dried-up bed of a stream, reminded Wolin of Spain. But when he looked up he saw trees covered with the light green beads of buds. The sky was pink, the setting sun veiled in mist. There might be the chance of a woodcock; there must be some about. The walleyed man was nervous when Wolin went for a walk by himself. There might still be some members of Kord's gang hiding in the forest and he wanted to give him a bodyguard. Wolin touched his revolver and began whistling a tune from an old musical comedy. In some of the village windows lights were appearing. The people would be sitting now at their rough tables around oil lamps, eating from bowls with wooden spoons. They would be frightened, talk in whispers. Wolin liked to look at night through the windows of other people's homes. The pleasure he got from it consisted in observing their complete ignorance that beyond the stream of the little life in which they swam there existed another, and that the crossing of the two streams was inevitable; destiny was waiting somewhere around the corner and its agents were people like himself who had acquired an understanding of its laws. Perhaps this was the same pleasure he felt when he bent over an anthill in the summer. There were paths running up to it black with the hurrying insects. Their feverish agitation was to him the epitome of blindness and madness. They found a piece of straw or a beetle's wing; they pulled at it; other ants arrived and pulled in the opposite direction; if the forces were equal the struggle lasted sometimes for several minutes. At last the object slowly began to move. And then, suddenly, the ants that had resisted joined those that were pulling. Weren't social struggles a repetition of precisely the same process? Those masses who always joined the victors? In tiny pits dug into the loose sand of the paths sat the grubs of ant lions. They waited unmoving, only the ends of their powerful mandibles showing. A busy ant would step on the edge of the pit, the sand slipped and it found itself on the bottom; one movement of the jaws immobilized it, and it slowly sank deeper and deeper, drawn down by a merciless force. Wolin was amused by the fact that the ants, indifferent to their fate, advanced along paths lined with hundreds of such pits. Sometimes he would even throw ants to the ant lions that had been less successful.

The files which awaited him were full of names and faces. His pits were working well. But now he preferred to think about the two volumes of Labiche he had succeeded in buying in Warsaw. They bore the stamp of a library which had been burned down. Labiche gave him a great deal of satisfaction; he got endless pleasure from the perfect inanity of the affairs with which Labiche's petty-bourgeois characters filled their time. The humor of inanity. The plot centered around some absurd complication: bed, petty ambitions, things like that. All this was played by actors, while the audience—men and women in the ridiculous costumes of the past century, themselves engrossed in such nonsense, for it was their life—burst into fits of laughter and applause. How anything could be built out of inanity and nothingness had always been a mystery to Wolin. He strongly suspected that neither humor nor tragedy was possible in the age to which he belonged. And this suspicion, as a matter of fact, was confirmed by the country where he had spent the war years. Humor and tragedy could exist there but only privately—shamefacedly and without justification. For people like that brave young fool, Gdula, tragedy was evidently accessible: an oppressed nation, defense of the country, heroism, and so forth.

Wolin heard the singing of a thrush. Quietly, so as not to frighten it, he began to stalk it among the first alder trees of the forest. *Turdus musicus.* In a thicket, not very high above the ground, there must be a nest plastered inside with clay, smooth as if made by a potter. The female bird would be warming blue eggs with rust-colored spots. He saw the bird at the top of a spruce. The song rang forth, ecstatic, in the evening light over the obscurity below. With head tilted back, Wolin tried to see the throbbing of the small throat from which these sounds came. Unchanged, just as in his childhood, strangers to history, submitting only to the laws of the eternal return.

13

TIME, FLOWING UNEVENLY as a river over boulders, began to gather momentum for Peter. Whether he wanted to or not, he had to find a place for himself in conditions which seemed transient and impermanent—though he thought with distaste that the provisional often proved to be the most permanent of all. It was warm; trees were in full leaf, and in the evening the light of the street lamps shone through them; orchestras were playing in the garden cafés of Lodz, where he now lived. The questions he kept asking himself were losing their acuteness, and not for himself alone. Fear, shame for the past, and shame for the future, were wrapped for nearly everybody in a soft protective layer so that no one could touch them. People moved about, overcome by the somnambulant return of life, by the very air of the first spring after the war, the greenness of the trees, the traffic in the streets. They treated the lies in the newspapers and official speeches as extraneous things of no importance; they were busy reorganizing their lives, settling down, trading, creating intrigues in which they could discharge the hatred that filled them and for which there was no permissible political outlet. A lot of alcohol was drunk; women were easy, as if they realized that the human body was perishable and that it was silly to curtail the pleasures of the flesh by the rigid application of moral standards.

Peter met Eve and their affair began without much in the way of preliminaries. They drank in Bunio's company, danced together, and then he took her home. The fact that her knees trembled when they kissed in the dark staircase filled him with pleasure. She often came to see him after the show. She was an actress and all through the war had worked as a waitress in a Warsaw restaurant, observing the ban on acting proclaimed by the underground actors' union. Petite and vivacious, she was full of a particular brand of humor, familiar under the German occupation, but new and fascinating to Peter. She told him, laughing, about her husband: "Not a bit of him left! Nothing but a wet spot! He rushed at that tank which blew up in the Old City!" It was a tank loaded with dynamite that the Germans had planted on the insurgents. It had been taken through the barricades to the Market Square in the Old City, and a wildly enthusiastic crowd of soldiers and children had gathered around it. When the driver left his seat and lifted the hood, the whole thing exploded and a few hundred people were killed; their heads and arms were found on the balconies of the surrounding houses and on roof tops. The way in which her husband met his death amused Eve, for some reason, just as a great many other events and circumstances amused her, not excluding the fact that Peter—who was now demobilized and wore civilian clothes—could have served in the Bolshevik army and could publish serious articles.

"But it *is* all a joke. You're not like this really. Everybody plays a part nowadays and nobody believes in anything. Agents call themselves a government. An army commanded by Russian officers is called Polish. All you can do is laugh."

For Peter, Eve was, among other things, a means of re-establishing a link with the theater. The atmosphere of unreality and magic; the smell of greasepaint; dressing-room doors which slammed just as one had caught a glimpse of a bare arm under a glaring light; gossip, rivalries—all this now took on for him an exceptional fascination, perhaps because it was a world apart, a refuge. In it he rediscovered some personal continuity; although he wished to obliterate a great deal in his own past, he was still rather proud of his "theatrical" period, which he thought of as not bad at all. To be honest, the sense of continuity was precarious, too, because the theater was a reminder of the passage of years. Theresa had got married and now had a three-year-old son. When they met again they looked at each other attentively. Her figure had not changed and she still had long slim legs; but her breasts, always full, were now overblown; she had wrinkles around her eyes and silver strands in her hair. When he called on her and found her ladling out soup, a housewife, maternal, he felt the strangeness of life. He was the same, yet not the same, and so was she. Before the war when he saw the plays in which she acted, his emotions were heightened by a ridiculous male pride. From the dark auditorium he would watch her elastic step as a Shakespearean queen or a romantic heroine in a high-waisted costume. The real mystery of the theater was for him the merging of the hieratic with the indecent: a fusion in which he also discovered the secret of human beings, capable of creating poems and philosophies amidst excrement and menses. He had experienced it most strongly one evening when they were in process of moving into a new apartment and had nowhere to go; he and Theresa were walking along the boulevards by the river and, overcome by a sudden desire, they made love leaning against a metal balustrade. An hour later, the august rhythm of the poetry she spoke, her slow movements as the heroine of a tragedy on the stage came as the supreme contrast, the denial of biological laws, as the pure artifice which is identical with art.

His friendship with Theresa meant much to him: sisterly, yet not entirely devoid of an erotic memory which could interpet a shade of tone, a movement of the lips, a small gesture. To Theresa he could talk about everything, while Eve accepted his indulgent and amused silences.

A thing which had worried Peter recurrently for the past few years was a dream, too shameful and hideous to bear alone. Such dreams tend to be forgotten, for the organism neutralizes them while assimilating them imperceptibly like poisons. However, Peter often traced out its details, unable to share them with anybody, and the dream was always present and always accusing. He decided against telling his mother about it. It would have been impossible. The only person in whom he could confide was Theresa; and this meant that he would have to reveal to her even more than in the old days of their intimacy. He longed to slough off this burden and to submit it to another's judgment, suspecting that his own judgment, although this was most unflattering to his ego, might be erroneous. He told Theresa that what mattered here was not the past; rather, it was his feeling that the memory of the dream, like a wandering bullet lodged in his flesh, might one day reach his heart. He asked her aid.

Telling the story now produced in him a new kind of shame. It was polished, composed of carefully rehearsed sentences designed to communicate the inexpressible clearness of recollection. He felt as if he stood before a sheet of dark water, which had seemed to conceal great depths and then suddenly appeared so shallow as hardly to cover his feet. He noticed that he was avoiding essentials and at one point started to digress at length on the treatment of scurvy. (In camp the prisoners had brewed an extract of pine needles because they had no other medicine.) He also justified himself beforehand by reducing the dream to the level of an ordinary starvation nightmare. Nothing more natural than to be obsessed with the thought of food, than that the memory of the veal cutlets with cranberry sauce which he liked as a child should flood him with delight as he dreamed of them. Stammering, he told Theresa of his hatred and despair in camp. For thousands and thousands of miles around there was only indifference, and behind was a world which didn't want to know anything about people like him; and if it did know, would probably say they were criminals who deserved all they got. "I had death in my heart. It was as if I was lying at the bottom of an abyss surrounded by enormous rocks. Without hope."

The dream was an escape from hunger and humiliation. He was walking down a street in a large city and the passers-by were giving way to him, taking off their caps, saluting him. He stopped and looked into the face of a man kneeling before him. It was his school chaplain, wearing a uniform: the same chaplain who used to send him out of class shouting: "Kwinto, you've an indecent grin on your face," when Peter asked awkward questions about Christian doctrine.

Connected in some mysterious way with the chaplain's homage was a great marble staircase, a white palace built in a Southern style. The smell of oranges. In a large hall Negroes in checked coats were playing billiards. Jazz and songs. Peter stood in front of a table piled with food and was filled with overwhelming ecstasy. He was eating with a realization that he would never be hungry again, that there was no threat from anywhere, that his cutlets with cranberry sauce would never be taken away from him.

The dream, above all, was a dream of complete security. Everything was permeated by a powerful and kindly presence and Peter felt such a surge of love that he cried. Love for Him who filled the space. He took Peter on His knees and encircled him with His arm. Stalin was growing, becoming enormous, lifting a tiny Peter up and up; they were floating through space. And Peter suddenly understood that this was God the Father, with his luminous triangle, eternal peace, happiness without end.

Peter told the dream clumsily. But the questions he asked Theresa had the violence of protests: "Why?" he kept repeating, "Why? Why are you responsible for what you really are? Can anybody say: 'I am myself' when he worships in spite of himself, worships what he hates?"

The trunks of trees outside the window were black against the glare of the sun and their cylindrical shapes had the incomparable density of things in the fullness of existence. The place where they sprang from the flat earth was a place of growth, of genesis, of the creation of form. Theresa sat with her chin resting on her hand, her hair smoothly brushed back from a slightly convex forehead. Her knees stretched the fabric of her dress; her foot, merely by resting on the floor, did something which was in itself significant. To be able to immobilize oneself and the whole universe known through the senses, to become nothing but perception and comprehension. But time still existed and desire, fear, insecurity—the whole shifting morass of change and movement in which nothing is tangible and nothing is clearly outlined; where nothing can be pointed at with a finger and isolated by the magic word: "This." Peter was never comfortable in the world of feelings and passions. He suspected that somewhere in the proliferating speculations called psychology there was inherent dishonesty. He did not allow himself to analyze the sentimental content of his relationship with Theresa. What he liked best in her was that, as in himself, there were clearly marked boundaries. From here to here is your territory, she seemed to say, you are welcome to it, it is your due. But apart from the moments of pure animality, there was nothing left to be changed into fondness, into the rubbing of cheek against cheek, into affectionate nicknames. Their conversations were very frank but steered clear of what was taboo. If you exposed your entrails, Theresa said, you began, without knowing it, to tell an endless series of lies. Now he was exposing a sizeable entrail of his own. The malice of "this great historical epoch" which equated, against men's wills, the private and individual with the universal and general, forced him to return by this indirect route to those depths which to him were always suspect.

14

IF THERESA, WHEN he had told her about the dream, had taken him by the hand and burst out laughing, he would have laughed too, and that would have been the end of it. But she remained serious.

"They push our heads down and make us swallow filth. It has its effects. I'm sorry for you."

She reached for a little suit she was making for her child, threaded a needle and, breaking the thread with her teeth, looked at Peter.

"What can I do? You've got to snap out of it by yourself. Try to tell me what you think the dream means and perhaps I'll be able to add something."

Peter was grateful for the opportunity to go on with his egotistical revelations. He rested his head against the cool wall behind his chair:

"It's not really clear to me." He started slowly, with long pauses between the sentences. "First of all, if a man's subjected to oppression—completely—he reaches a limit where what he hates turns into an object of worship. He doesn't want to admit it: it's very unpleasant. But the only salvation seems to be to move closer to the center of strength than anybody else, closer to the source of grace and warmth. Perhaps I'm very odd in being so twisted and mixed up. At school that chaplain tormented me, but I loved him simply because he was a single-minded fanatic. Perhap this sort of attitude's really quite common. And then, I've always found it difficult to accept the fact that I'm a separate being, that I've got to make decisions. All my revolts sprang from an inarticulate desire for an impossible unity, for some sort of fusion with other people. I revolted because there was something missing in everybody around me—they weren't strong enough to make me respect their strength or their intelligence—it's the same thing, two sides of the same coin. But it's pretty horrible, a ghastly indictment against me. Who am I? I want truth. But whatever truth I find's always too unconvincing to stand up—against them. In the dream even God was taken from me. Identically the same."

Theresa listened while she went on sewing.

"Do you know what you're doing now?" she asked. "You're justifying your fatalism."

When he didn't reply she added:

"The dream's a warning."

"A warning?"

"Most important of all is what happened to your father. And the fact that you're an orphan. They killed your father, so they seem all-powerful to you."

It would be silly to say any more. "Stop thinking about it. The dream was a warning. You were in danger of being hypnotized by your own self-abasement. It's a good thing you told me about it. You needn't tell anybody else."

Peter too thought that he had done the right thing. Theresa's words surprised him. It was as though he had come across something quite obvious, something he had always known, though he had never put it into words before. Until now, he hadn't connected his father with the dream, though the fact that his father had been killed fighting them made him more ashamed of his own belief in their ultimate victory. Now he saw the problem in a different light. The loss of his father was the hidden reason for his weakness. And what about the others who cling to the collective faith, to the warmth of the beehive; in their case, too, did it stem from some early trauma? From a death, or from something less—the loss of respect for parents, events coming too fast one upon the other, and causing a rift between generations, an estrangement in the home? If what Theresa said was true, the dream was meant not to condemn but to warn. It should be counted among the intuitions which served his mother and sometimes himself so well. It wasn't, after all, a hateful aberration—something to conceal and be ashamed of.

And he saw more clearly now why he was attracted to Artym: he was looking for a paraclete, a guide to help him when he was assailed by doubts. As in his childhood, he was simply longing for a large tree. Artym was very old, he had survived the war, and even his apartment in a suburb of Warsaw was undamaged. But Peter had not yet called on him, he was too frightened. Artym belonged to the "intransigent" Socialists. The fact that he was left alone was probably due to his eminent name—it was always better not to create martyrs—and his great age. Because Peter was cultivating Baruga and had, without permitting himself to believe in them, plans for a journey abroad, it would be bad if his friendship with Artym were noted. Artym might well be under observation. After his conversation with Theresa, Peter decided to call on Artym after all.

15

THE BROAD VISTULA flowed in the fiery heat
of the first summer days, its waters muddy with sand
from its bed. Across the river rose the ravaged city,
incongruous under the cheerful skies. The surface of
the water, accustomed already to the ruined bridges,
formed the same long eddies around them. Further
along, beyond the last bridge, the broad beaches below
the willows were now deserted. In the old days at this
time of the year a motley crowd used to fill them.
There used to be the blaring of radios and the shouts
of ice-cream sellers.

Seal walked around heaps of barbed wire and frag-
ments of sheet metal riddled with bullets. He took a
long walk every day out to spots from which he could
see the ragged bluish skyline of Warsaw. He revisited
again the places where in his schooldays he had played
truant with his friends. He stretched himself on the
sand, exposing his naked body to the sun. This was
one of his greatest pleasures. It made his thoughts
bearable, deprived them somehow of their inevitability.
Slowly he entered the river; he swam and then floated
on his back, abandoning himself to the current and
letting it carry him to a sandbank. He was slightly
ashamed of being able to enjoy the light and the
water as much as he used to. His pleasure was mixed
with a feeling of guilt, but he did enjoy it, and he told
himself that there was no real reason why he shouldn't,
and that it was silly to ask too much of oneself.

When he had returned to Warsaw he took lodgings with the family of a railwayman he used to know in Praga. He had to make a living somehow but for the time being this had taken care of itself. Darevicz, one of the Socialist leaders he had run into, gave him two hundred dollars. Seal didn't want to accept it, but Darevicz shrugged his shoulders and said that it wasn't his and that he didn't know what to do with it. He belonged to a group of Socialists who considered the new authorities' invitation to collaborate with them to be nothing but a trap and who predicted a sad end for the people now engaged in organizing the "legal" Socialist party. Since he was in personal danger because of his views, he no longer slept at home.

Seal could not define precisely what the new way of life was. He had never before experienced anything Eastern. It defied description, was like air, an aura, a presence which, apart from its material manifestations, was invisible to the eye. All during his trip home from camp, Seal had been convinced that he was moving toward a new occupation. Five years passed under the Nazi terror had accustomed him to this kind of life, and he did not much care. But this was different from what he had known before. They could throw him into prison as a former soldier of the Home Army. They were arresting many people. But that wasn't what disturbed him. In the eyes of all the people he knew, in the eyes of everyone he met in the street, he saw fear. And this fear was different, new: it was not a fear of immediate dangers, it was more like the mysterious menace, the taboo-ridden terror, which hangs over primitive tribes. Their lips pronounced formulas that were always the same, as confused as their feelings: "This is only the beginning." In years past you did, of course, insure yourself as much as you could against danger: with false documents, fictitious labor cards. But now people were rushing to join the Party, taking on safe jobs, planning, preparing themselves against some unimaginable Day of Judgment. A movement of their eyes, a sudden blush, an unexpected bowing of the head, betrayed the inner chaos and anguish that inspired their conduct. Former comrades of his clandestine organization had explained to Seal that the work of the Socialists was very important now and that he should join the "legal" party. They boasted that they were going to show the Communists who were the real bosses in the country and who had the masses behind them. After some reflection, Seal said no. Somehow it rang false. He preferred the attitude of his friend the railwayman who showed him his newly acquired Communist Party card and winked.

Seal had plenty of leisure. His skin was getting brown and the rhythm of the river remained in him like the fluid essence of the world. Even in fine weather the Vistula preserved its sadness. Unregulated, it cut new beds in the sandy soil, spreading its waters capriciously over the empty plain. Now there were no barges of ballast, no fishermen's boats, no canoes. Herons, emboldened by the absence of man, waded in the shallows.

Seal could not decide what to do with himself. In the Vistula he sought purification and baptism—for what? For a long time he had been postponing his visit to the ruins of the Old City. Perhaps he had been afraid to go there alone. Talking to a friend about some of the university professors, he learned that Gil was in Warsaw and asked for his address.

The professor now lived in a distant southern suburb. The villas, their windows boarded up with plywood, stood among masses of weeds through which narrow paths had been trodden. The meeting was awkward. Seal stammered that he had been with Joanna during the rising against the Nazis and would like to . . . that he thought . . . He saw in front of him a tall, gaunt man, on whose once shaven head the newly growing hair stood up on end. He had unkempt, bushy eyebrows and a mouth twisted into an expression of stubbornness. Seal was shifting from one foot to another, trying in vain to find a family resemblance between father and daughter. The whole idea of going to see Gil suddenly seemed quite futile. But the expression of the older man's eyes—clear, detached from himself and his surroundings—was familiar. It gave him a strange pang of pain. "Joanna . . . I'm looking for her grave. Perhaps you know something?" the professor asked.

To get to that house they had to go clear across Warsaw. After they had passed a few streets in which there was a little traffic, their steps began to ring and echo in the silence of dead squares. The rattling of a small cart and the clop-clop of the wooden shoes of two children who were pulling it echoed from the burnt-out walls. With spades on their shoulders, the two men made their way through the molehills of the Old City. With great difficulty Seal found the ruins of the house. He stood in what had been the courtyard

211

and could not understand the connection between what he had once seen and lived through and what he now had to think of as reality. He thought that everything must come from inside man and not from outside. Eskimos or Lapps live in a country where there is nothing—no plants, no trees. And simply because they were human beings it was filled with color and life for them.

His expedition with Gil and the job they did was something which afterwards he preferred to forget. They found Joanna's body on the third day, when their suits reeked with the stink of corpses. Gil, at any rate, was sure that the body was his daughter's. Seal wanted to tell him about Joanna but found he had very little to say. So he limited himself to facts. He mentioned Osman and how she went with him to the top of the house, and he told of Father Ignatius's visit. He did not mention the friction between Bertrand and Father Ignatius, but he did not hide his own dislike of the priest.

Gil asked him if Joanna had confessed. From the tone of his voice Seal could not guess if he hoped for a yes or a no. He himself thought about it for the first time. He did not know. "Bertrand," he added, for he felt bound to say so, "was my friend. A logician and a positivist. Joanna respected him a lot." Gil nodded. Contact with the professor was difficult. He embarrassed Seal, who never knew what he was really thinking, but there sprang up between them, in spite of the difference in their ages, something like silent comradeship.

Hidden in the rushes by the river, Seal sometimes

wept a little, from sheer loneliness. This whole useless life. He tried to imagine what Bertrand would have done—Bertrand, so incisive, the person you could always rely on. The shameful business of Gdula preyed on his mind most of all because it was a betrayal of Bertrand's good opinion of him. He decided to make that betrayal good, but every possible way of doing so seemed equally hopeless. By taking part in nothing, by denying everything, he was choosing the path of a hermit.

One day, pushing aside the rushes, he saw a group of young men and girls. They were all completely naked. They were playing cards. By their nakedness, by the lazy movements with which they shuffled and dealt their cards in the emptiness of suspended time, they demonstrated their complete indifference to communal laws, customs, tasks, problems of the past and future. Duty, convictions, the sacrifice of their own lives were all far behind them. They were alive and that was all. If Seal were to go up to them and say that, like them, he was a soldier of this shattered city, they would look up, invite him with a gesture to join in, and deal him a hand. Letting the rushes go and quietly moving away, he retained an impression of places where, among traces of transient civilizations, on the banks of flowing rivers through deserted lands, there lived small groups of people ignorant of each other's existence, equally hostile to what had been and what would be. He was like them; there were many of them; but they would lead to nothing.

16

WHEN HE CALLED on Artym the second time, Peter encountered a stranger. A young man with a mourning band on the sleeve of his grubby linen jacket rose uncertainly from an armchair; his back was humped, his long arms hung down clumsily; his tanned face reminded Peter of the faces of Warsaw street urchins before the war, narrow and ironical; but there was no gayety in it. The two men looked at each other fixedly. Peter felt uncomfortable. If he was to see Artym at all it was better to see him alone.

Artym guessed their misgivings: "You must get acquainted. It's all right. You can trust each other completely. If I have you both here together it's because I'm sure of you both. Seal—Cisovski, who fought in the rising—Kwinto, back from Russia."

Artym had a white beard which lay flat on his chest. He spoke softly as people who have weak hearts often do. Retired long ago from active political life, he remained a legend: of past struggles of the workers against Czarism, of faith in progress, in a European community of nations. In Artym's home, between walls stacked to the ceiling with books, Peter felt that he was on an island where truth and frankness were obligatory. These isolated islands—his mother, Theresa, Artym—were indispensable to his existence. Yet he could not get any help from Artym in his personal arguments against necessity. There was no bitterness in what the old man said, nor did he mitigate his pessimistic opinions for didactic purposes. The language he used carried one into a world whose outlines were blurred by the mist of distance.

"Our anti-Trinitarians carried wooden sabers to manifest their absolute pacifism," he said. "And that happened in the bloodthirsty sixteenth century. They disputed whether a Christian could hold public office, because every office was an office of the sword. At that time the might of Ivan the Terrible was growing in the East. Now, we resorted to violence against the Czarist police, but our ideal of the future was as non-violent as that of those humanists. We believed that the people themselves would recognize who had served them well. Today our people, for nationalistic reasons, are opposing the successors of Ivan. But has not a trace of our work, of our vanquished dream, been preserved in their distaste for oppression?"

"Dialectics!" he shrugged his shoulders. "Marx didn't teach that the understanding of facts should be prevented by force. I don't know if you ever heard of a man called Machajski. One of our Socialists. That was a long time ago, in my youth. The Czar's government had him deported to Siberia. He was the author of only one small booklet, published in Russian, in which he expounded his theory. According to him, when you say that the proletariat makes a revolution, this really means that revolution is being made by intellectuals looking for their place in the social organism. You know, there's a grain of truth in that. Look at the madness of the Russian intelligentsia, a suicidal madness. Like the sexual attraction of a male spider to the female that will devour him afterwards.

Look at the backward countries, at India, China. The masses are apathetic there. But let a man learn to read, taste some knowledge, go to a university, and he becomes a Stalinist. This seems to him obvious and logical. The great snare of the twentieth century. If it's scientifically precise and looks good on paper why not wish for it, why not put it into practice? When the sorcerer's apprentice begins to wonder about demonism it's too late: he's already the servant of the demon he liberated."

Artym did not spare the Socialists either. "For you all this is little short of mythology. For my generation the dispute was fundamental: between those who wanted socialism and independence and people like Rosa Luxemburg who were against the separation from Russia of the countries conquered by the Czars. Yet those countries severed themselves—or most of them did. The Ukraine stayed in. So did Georgia. This was our triumph, here in Poland, and at the same time our failure. Because internationalism has been sacrificed and the new Czarism of the Bolsheviks has proved us right. In accepting national unity, we disrupted ourselves from within. And the Socialist parties, those creations of the nineteenth century, have lasted long enough to see the approaching end of all politics. What were the Socialists doing before the war? In the days of dictatorships, rabid nationalism, racialism, black reaction? Nothing at all outside their own ranks and the workers' universities—or at any rate nothing but word-spinning. Today we're seeing the posthumous triumph of those of our Social Democrats who wanted to follow the Russians, those fathers of the Communist Party. And at the same time their defeat. And now the latest spectacle—a new "legal" Socialist party. It must be part of the preparations for a withdrawal, for a slow undermining of the program of workers' democracy and independence which has been in force up to now. As for myself, you can be quite sure that I'm not going to lend a hand."

It was no use asking Artym for advice. "Can one measure an individual destiny with a slide rule?" he would ask. "Is it the duty of all Christians to take up arms and kill Communists? And if somebody loves his country, should he imitate the Russian aristocrats who became taxi-drivers in Paris? Or those Polish officers, attorneys, judges, lawyers, dignitaries who will wash dishes in the hotels of London and New York waiting, year in, year out, to return to their former positions— something which will never happen. Can you say to anyone: 'Work here, with the Socialists or the peasants,' when you know in advance that in the end this must either lead him to orthodox Stalinism, if he behaves himself, or to prison, if he doesn't?"

Peter disagreed. The time factor, he said, was important. Time: if the process of change was as slow as seemed likely, all sorts of unexpected formulas could emerge, because by saying they wanted to try new methods and new formulas, even by awakening the hope that they would be introduced, the Communist Party itself was exposed to the current of change.

Artym shook his head; his long hands rested on his knees.

"Perhaps. I don't want to be a prophet. For a number of years a number of people may—perhaps—be successful at that game. Provided they realize that these new methods are nothing but tactical expedients. I know the history of the Ukraine. Believe me, things there were exactly the same at the beginning."

"If I openly condemn any compromise with them on the part of the Socialists," Artym said, "it's because I can't do otherwise. I'm forced by my whole past life. Let them lock me up if they want to. I've very little time left, anyway. But this isn't any criterion. Everybody's got to decide according to his own conscience how he must act to preserve some decency. All the reactionaries among the *émigrés* will, of course, appropriate to themselves the monopoly of being 'pure.' They'll try to forget what they've done—or rather what they haven't done. According to them, whoever cares only for his own money is always innocent. No, today everybody must not only make a choice, but also a choice within a choice."

When they left Artym's together, Cisovski, who had hardly spoken before, said, as though addressing the air: "We can't count on anybody. We're alone." Peter understood; it was the same bitter disappointment he had felt himself when listening to Artym. As Julian Halpern would have said, it was stagecoach travel in the age of airplanes.

Peter was not anxious to unmask himself. He knew that sooner or later information about opinions expressed even in the circle of one's closest friends reached in some mysterious way the ears of those who wanted to know. The fact that he was received by Artym together with Seal and took part in the conversation made them confederates. From then on he made friends with Seal, though it was not easy for him. He always had some difficulty in establishing contact with people younger than himself. Moreover he felt like a man groping blindly in a dark room and Seal was even more helpless than he was. He asked questions which to Peter seemed childish. And if the questions touched on Peter's experiences in Russia, Peter was unable to overcome his habit of silence and could answer only in monosyllables. Seal, too, kept to himself a number of his personal affairs. He never spoke of his wife, and at any mention of the rising he became silent, tense, and only occasionally uttered a word of contempt about the men who had given the order to start it. Peter found in him a grim ardor, a suppressed need for enthusiasm, and he thought that Seal, more easily than he, could become a fanatical adherent of the Eastern doctrine—should he ever experience that sudden illumination which Peter knew from his observation of other people and which he thought must be like the illumination of a drug addict who can see in a plain wall or in a nail the extraordinary harmony of a super-logic of the universe. But Seal, not finding at Artym's what he had been looking for, drew one conclusion from his disappointment—that he should reject everything that was happening, without considering whether such a negation was stupid or wise, laudable or discreditable. He seemed to believe that some underground activity was possible. And he answered Peter's sceptical remarks by saying that it didn't matter how long such activity could be effective.

One day, towards the end of the summer, Seal confided to Peter that he had a problem: it was necessary to organize Darevicz's escape abroad. Reliable documents were needed—just in case—because the chaos in the Western Territories facilitated transit to Germany. Peter had heard a great deal about Darevicz's courage under the Nazi occupation. He produced some passes authorizing him to move about freely in the frontier zone which he had just received because he was to visit the area near the Oder and write a series of articles.

"Take these. Remember to change the name. If I'm asked, I'll tell them I've lost the papers. But remember that the Russians don't take much notice of these passes. It's safer not to overrate their respect for legality."

Having done it, he realized immediately that his action was unwise. Not for nothing was it said—over there—that you were never out of danger while you had friends.

17

IN THE PRISONS which he had so far seen from the inside, Michael had become used to bearing almost everything—except the stench. Now he breathed the incomparably exotic scent of eau de cologne, which emanated from the man whose smoothly combed hair glistened in the lamplight. He assessed his adversary and stuck his nails into the edge of his chair. This was only his third interrogation in the course of several months. From the first and second he had emerged victorious—or so he thought. Victory had nothing to do with the result—although the result was rather good, too. He had succeeded at the time in not loosening, even for a moment, that inner tension which could be undermined by fear. Concentrating on the one focal point which radiated warmth somewhere inside him, he had sat quietly while the fat Russian on the other side of the table screamed curses at him. He had said that he didn't understand Russian. The conversation was later resumed through an interpreter. Michael decided to go the whole hog. He entrusted himself to his instinctive feel of the situation, which told him that the only means of defense was surprise. Was he a fascist? Yes, he was. Had he published papers? Yes, he had. He preferred to exaggerate the role he had played, presenting a consciously demoniac picture of himself. That first test had been a clash of two different human atmospheres; he could not allow himself to be bullied and admit the superiority of the other man.

The second interrogation was, he thought, a proof that he had won the first round: the new NKVD man seemed to be of higher rank than the first one. He conducted long political discussions in German with him, in a toneless voice, in order not to disturb his surface calm, stressed rather aggressively the difficulties which a Russian administration over half of Europe would encounter. If he was going to die, it was better to die in style. At the same time he guessed that the further away he got from the normal run of cases with which the Russians had to deal, and the more specialized his case could become, the better it would be for him.

Now he was faced by this elegent creature. The gestures with which he moved the lamps on the table were harmonious. The light directed at Michael's face was not glaring. Michael rocked from side to side, trying to find a rhythm inside himself—the rhythm of a leisurely circling round a point of light located somewhere in his stomach, his heart, or perhaps in space above his head. The gray eyes of the investigator looked towards him. A cool customer, Michael thought.

"Michael Kamienski." Wolin's hand was opening a thick file. "We know everything about you. Your own units of the National Armed Forces withdrew with the German army. That was the net result of your activity. The absolute logic of sliding down a slope. How did you avoid being captured by the Germans after the rising?"

"I didn't want to be deported to Germany. Not even as a prisoner of war. I left Warsaw with a crowd of civilians. Doctors I knew got me out of the processing camp." Michael folded his hands on his knees. He was preparing fictitious names should the man ask him about it.

"And later?"

"I stayed at Podkova Lesna. The idea of being an *émigré* repelled me."

That was true. His political associates tried to induce him to cross to the West before the Russians arrived. Father Ignatius, in spite of rumors that he had been killed in the Old City, re-emerged and accused him of lack of realism. In his view, they had to prepare for a new war in the immediate future. Father

222

Ignatius himself had set out towards Prague and Vienna.

"Why?"

Michael was tracing his inward circles. Under the collar of his adversary's khaki tunic, he could see the whiteness of his silk shirt. He was filled with longing for a bath and for clean underwear. He could smell the odor of his unwashed body encased in his crumpled suit, and he was conscious of the roughness of his unshaven cheeks. He answered slowly:

"Because it would be contrary to my estimate of the situation. We won't gain anything by counting on the British and Americans. For them we're an object to trade with, as other nations are. I've never been an adherent of their businessman's democracy. The laws of merchants are not laws for times like these."

"So you admit your defeat?"

Under the words a clash of currents. Michael kept his head up. They looked each other in the eyes.

"Your defeat will come. Maybe from the side least expected by you or by me."

The man behind the lamp lit a cigarette. Michael greedily inhaled the smoke curling towards him. The man, blowing out the match, said:

"Ah, a mystical faith. Admirable. The only possible way of dreaming about a resurrection of the Middle Ages. I know. A cathedral, and all around it small houses inhabited by craftsmen. Order. Each man in his place. By hereditary right. A cobbler with cobblers, a Jew with the Jews in the ghetto. A little bit of Berdyaev. A little bit of T. S. Eliot. Enchanting."

Who was this man? Michael wondered. How many

223

of his kind have they got to serve them loyally? His accent was pure. He didn't speak Polish with a Russian singsong.

The man spoke through clenched teeth:

"The price of putting the clock back is high. Blood. Here, on your hands."

For a moment Michael waited.

"Your longing for order is no less fantastic than ours. A distaste for the law of barter. For the rule of money. And blood."

The man seemed amused by this reply. His mouth curled into a mischievous smile.

"If I understand you rightly, this means that you find similarities between us and yourselves?"

Michael shook his head.

"I am not a Marxist."

"Most certainly not," said Wolin slowly and ironically. "You have advocated the necessity of shaking off the influence of foreign capitalists while taking money from your own local capitalists. We, by one decree, have put an end to the country's being sucked clean by dividends which go abroad, and by the people who had supported you. Now you're not putting any bets on the British and Americans. By this you seem to imply that any changes here will be along our lines. Is this so?"

"You are hated by everybody. Forced consent is no real consent."

"I see," the man propped his face on his hands. "You are putting your money on internal resistance. And if you were to give some advice to a man who in some measure feels responsible for the fate of this

224

country, to a politician, what would you advise? Under our system conspiracy is impossible. You know that. Incitement to assassination means only a multiplication of victims. We're putting the railways and factories back into operation. We've recovered the Western Territories which had once been Slav as far as Berlin—and that, if I'm not mistaken, was part of your program during the war. And these lands can only be defended by us. Well then?"

Michael, absorbed by his circling world, felt the hardness of his chair.

"You yourselves provoked assassinations. Incitement like that is nonsensical. But your real objective is philosophic not economic. And there you'll encounter resistance."

Wolin was turning over the pages of the file.

"Your trial is looking quite promising. A show trial, to teach people that the way of fascism is the way of national treason. Before the war you went to Hamburg to establish contacts. You believed that there, in Germany and Italy, were the signposts of history. You published eulogies of Mussolini. Later, you fought against the Germans. In appearance. At the same time you used them to liquidate Jews and people suspected of leftist opinions. Even some of those in the service of the London government. We'll be able to put it all together the right way."

"I've never approved of murders committed by fools."

Wolin said coolly:

"You even helped to hide Jews? Yes? But according to us a man is responsible for the consequences of his

225

words. According to us, even Nietsche is responsible, though he didn't know what use would be made of him."

Closing the file with a swift gesture and leaning back in his chair, he said suddenly:

"In spite of all this, we might be prepared to let you go. It depends entirely on you. On whether you accept our conditions."

The warm light lay on Michael's face. He closed his eyes and asked in a scarcely audible voice:

"What are your conditions?"

Wolin's voice penetrated to Michael's center of balance. He saw the movement of the scales: yes, no; yes, no.

"We're not impractical enough to ask for too much. We know your value. What we expect is a strict minimum. You didn't want to go into exile. Very well. Now draw your own conclusions. Our condition is that you should accept the existing order of things and help us thereby to lessen the number of victims. We'll give you the opportunity to publish a paper."

Michael, not opening his eyes, lifted his chin and said:

"If you accept my conditions."

"Speak up." There was something like curiosity in Wolin's voice.

"The recognition of the existing order of affairs is not false on my part. It is a realistic assessment. On the other hand, I do not recognize your philosophy and I shall always make that clear. I am a Catholic."

"The meaning of that word is not at all clear today," said Wolin. "It was clear as long as a man could include dogmas in his picture of the world. He can't do that today. From Catholicism, at least here in this country, you have derived—or thought you derived—your political conceptions. But in reality it was from your political calculations that you deduced the need for Catholicism."

"Your weakness lies in refusing to take intangible things into account." Michael looked up with half-closed lids. "There has been a thousand years of Catholicism here, and a nation which denies its tradition loses its spiritual life. It's a question of keeping faith."

"It comes to the same thing. A purely pragmatic justification of religion." Wolin blew on his palm. "That's all that's left of metaphysics. But we won't quarrel. Do you think we want you to declare yourself one of us? On the contrary. We've no intention of touching Catholicism. Your activities should have convinced you that it's possible to accept revolution while maintaining your own private opinions."

Michael was silent. He was beset by the endless complications of the decision facing him. He tried to measure them and to project them into the future. The course of his life? His good name?

The other man, as if guessing this, said:

"The question of what's called 'purity' is the preserve today of people who simply refuse to see clearly. Whoever acts ceases to be pure. You'll save the lives of many young men. Instead of despair and suicide, they'll find an objective and a hope. The lives of other people do matter to you as a Christian, I suppose?"

"Let's say I'm a realist," Michael arched his large

back. "But people like me will be a tiny minority among the Catholics. The condition I make is that you should not force me to publish pronouncements that would compromise me in the eyes of other Catholics. That you leave me a free hand within the framework of my estimate of the state of affairs."

Wolin held out his cigarette case to him and gave him a light. Inhaling, Michael saw his old self speaking at meetings. A decent acceptance of defeat was after all a kind of courage.

"Let's put our cards on the table," said the inquisitor. "You will lend us your name. In exchange, you will be able to practice spiritual resistance quite legally. At this moment, we're sure of victory anyway. We might test our forces. Your Nietzsche understood, somewhat late in the day, that God was dead. Hegel's trinity was derived from your Catholic Trinity. And this was more important than the attacks of anti-Trinitarians. Our goal is to find people who, while not themselves Marxists, are ready to support the economic reconstruction of the country. As for the rest, you'll play for time. And so will we. It's in our interests to give you a free hand. Is this enough?"

A man is born, walks in short trousers, reads about Indians, then about history—poisonings, stabbings, bargains, and intrigues—not knowing the bitterness his own century may prepare for him. Conscious of the years of darkness in front of him, Michael said:

"All right."

"The fact that we were able to reach an understanding is not accidental." Wolin looked at him earnestly. "You've always understood that if you want to change

228

the world you can't use the falsehoods of the parliamentary system and that the liberal ideas of merchants were only a transient ripple on the tide of progress. In a few days you will be discharged. Comrade Baruga is now organizing the press. He'll give you an allocation of paper and make arrangements about printing."

18

THE RIDERS REIN in their horses and stop. Below them a great land, delivered to their power. They look at rivers shining in the sun, at the ruins of ravaged cities quiet in the bluish mist. In the valleys tiny people come and go, unconscious of their destiny. On round hills proud castles brandish their towers at the sky. From those castles they will rule. Pointing with the tips of their swords, they show each other where they plan to build new cities, new magnificent monuments, dams, arches. They know that at a sign from them human swarms will go to work. Half-naked, in rhythmical effort, they will carry beams and great hewn stones. Over their daily toil, over the meaningless nonsense of their lives, an idea—shrewd, imperious, sharpened by argument—will bear undisputed rule.

It was a picture conjured up for Peter by Julian's words. He had drawn closer again to his old friend in spite of Theresa's dislike and distrust of him. And he had stopped seeing Seal, perhaps because of Darevicz, who had succeeded in getting abroad. Julian

229

spoke of happiness: of the happiness felt by people whose ears were tuned to the music of history. Peter was flattered by the fact that he was included by Julian amongst those who knew. He rejected contemptuously the majority of their acquaintances, retaining only an inner circle of the initiated. He needed security— Julian offered it to him as one whose life would consist of wielding power and beneath whose feet the earth would lie prostrate. Peter, confused by what he had seen in the past and by what he saw now, longed for a barrier to separate him from the masses that were merely the passive objects of historical processes. In the vision created by Julian's words, the arms of the peasant woman whose son was being taken away from her were receding into the distance, into the regions of the inevitable where, seen remotely, individual destiny became pale—completed, no matter how, by old age, imprisonment, execution, an accident. Julian, pleased that he had regained his influence over Peter, played up to the feudal past of Peter's family. Peter's origins, he used to say, ought to be a safeguard against excessive sentimentality. A time was coming when the intellectuals could settle their scores with the bourgeoisie. The harmless cranks, the *poètes maudits,* had iron gauntlets on their hands now. The future lay before them, basking in the sun. Ruling over the executioners, over their underlings, in bright rooms in lofty castles, a group of intellectuals was about to turn the dream of Faust into reality.

The swing of the pendulum which had brought Peter to Artym was now taking him in the opposite direction. He published a number of articles that were

230

less moderate than before. And just then, when he had ceased to hope for it, it happened: Baruga told him that he would be sent to Paris.

Peter was conscious that the estimate of a man's "reliability" was based, under the system, on hardly perceptible signs: on the general aura which emanated from the person being assessed. The fact that the chance of a trip to Paris came during his Julian phase was not accidental: the one thing was connected with the other. Peter asked himself if his instinct had helped him again—that same instinct which stage-managed so many of his interior comedies. Instead of receiving the news about Paris calmly, he suddenly felt afraid, for he had lately become almost reconciled and had begun to find his place among the conquerors. Baruga liked to make noble gestures, but it was a far cry from a noble gesture to the issuance of a passport. Peter's fears increased when he began to visit the Ministry of Foreign Affairs. In the averted eyes of the new civil servants, in their shifty looks, was the same expression as there was in the eyes of the strangely dressed individuals who waited for an interview for hours on end; they walked nervously along the dirty corridors, cracking their fingers. Fear. All of them— this was fairly clear—were desperately playing, each in his own way, for the stake of release from the trap. The case of Peter's passport dragged on. In the non-committal promises of the secretary on whom he called regularly every week he could detect a self-satisfied scepticism.

Julian tried to reassure him. "Of course you'll go. It'll do you good. You'll see that in the West there's nothing your hands or spirit can cling to. You're not a half-wit. No one gives up a kingdom for a mess of pottage. You're with us. Whoever's with us will have everything. Money—which for people like us doesn't matter—books, travel. You can see for yourself. You want to travel and you do travel. And from there you'll see everything more clearly than from here."

But hope was already destroying Peter's tenuous equilibrium, bringing to the surface too many suppressed desires. It was the repetition in a new context of a recurring pattern in his life. In the past, when he had found himself in the Soviet zone in 1939, he wanted to escape—even though it meant living under the German occupation—to buy time and to decide, for once and all, what he did believe. He could not now visualize himself strolling along the streets of Paris: what sort of person would he be there? Perhaps the changed human atmosphere all round him would suddenly tear away the veils that concealed reality. The journey would be a test to see whether, as he sometimes suspected, he had not simply been sick since 1939. He would have to check the reality of what seemed real. And his fear sprang from the memory of his arrest in 1939: if certain constant elements were always repeated, now, at the last moment, something similar might happen again.

To belong to a dominant caste—was there in this frightening world any other means of averting danger? Could you achieve victory over time only by standing on a mountain top and surveying the kingdoms of the world and saying: "All this is ours"? Peter did not reject that temptation. He still delayed the affirmation,

232

like a man who postpones an important decision when running a temperature. He waited. And at night he tossed and turned, remembering the malicious smile of one man, the ironical remark of another—did they mean, he wondered, that no passport would be issued.

Meanwhile, he heard that Winter had been appointed second secretary to the embassy in Paris.

19

MEN IN RAGGED suits hooked steel cables around the sharp corners of walls with the help of poles. Then, taking a firm hold on the cables, they pulled, singing out: "Ho-oop, Ho, Ho-oop." And the wall would at last suddenly collapse, raising great clouds of dust. To clear away the debris they used makeshift drays, long planks laid on wheels and pulled by a single horse. Groups of men and women with spades were busy among the ruins, removing rubble to repair the surface of the streets.

Seal spent his days now working in the ruins of Warsaw. In places where as a child he had looked every day at toy soldiers in a shopwindow, at a pastry shop, at the mysterious lights of a movie, where later he used to buy flowers for Catherine, where they had bought together, with money they had saved, a warm jacket for her—he now bent over his spade, putting aside the intact bricks, loading a wagon with debris full of touching little scraps of memory, a money box, a tin soldier, ridiculous objects less destructible than human beings or a city. At noon, sitting down with the others in the cold autumn breeze, he would eat the lunch he had brought from home in the morning. Sometimes one of the workmen would produce a quart of vodka and uncork it by hitting the bottom of the bottle with his palm; then they would all take nips, passing the bottle from hand to hand. He felt at ease with these people, who were like those he had grown up among in a poor street near the river. Their cynical sense of humor was familiar to him and so was their understanding of human affairs, which they could express in a few words. By spitting, they emphasized their views on the absurdity of the destruction, on a new government taking over and beginning reconstruction, on the Russians, the secret police, the necessity for working without any equipment or machinery. Yet they felt that the city had to be rebuilt. With expert knowledge they discussed which streetcar routes would be restored first, which district would get water and electricity, where the ruins would have to be razed to the ground so that new houses could be built some day. They kept silent about many things in their past and did not disclose their thoughts on the future. They clung to a measurable, visible task—patriots of a desert which for them continued to conceal both a past and a future life. Seal told himself that he ought to stay with these people. Perhaps in this daily physical toil to achieve something useful for other people he could expiate his sins. Everything else could only deceive. He was pleased that Darevicz had been successful in getting abroad, but Darevicz was the only man who had tried to hold together the remains of their organization.

Since his departure all the links had broken, and everybody went his own way. Artym was too old. Seal blamed himself for having been too reticent with Peter, though he had needed his friendship so much. He ascribed to his ill luck the fact that Peter had suddenly ceased to see him. Nothing would ever come of his dream of having someone near to his heart.

At dusk he used to return to Praga across the pontoon bridge, to eat the supper served by the wife of his friend the railwayman; in bed, he would try to study a textbook on botany and fall asleep after the first few sentences.

One evening, as he entered the dark staircase of his house, he felt that there was someone else there. He wanted to avoid the man. A flashlight shone in his face. "Excuse me," said a thick voice, "are you citizen Cisovski? Will you come with us." There were two of them in civilian clothes. In front of a neighboring house a jeep was waiting with its lights switched off. They started, the wind tugged at Seal's flannel scarf. The first snow of the season was falling, the flakes felt cool against his face. Perhaps it was best this way, he thought. And perhaps it didn't matter anyhow.

20

WOLIN GLANCED THROUGH the papers.

"These punch-drunk opposition Socialists are the most dangerous pests left. I see, Darevicz's escape. Cisovski. Home Army, of course. We don't need him for the moment, but he might come in useful later.

Keep him locked up for the time being. Take his deposition."

Wolin's room was not far from the office of the Minister of Public Security. He called the whole building the "clinic"—both patients and staff provided interesting material for his psychological observations.

His assistant, a small hunchback with glasses, handed him a piece of paper.

"Comrade, here's an informer's report on Cisovski."

Wolin read it attentively.

"Peter Kwinto? I've always said that we shouldn't let people like him get out. He was friendly with Cisovski. Do you think he's going abroad to escape? This report's an intelligent piece of work. It might be worth following up."

In approving Kwinto's departure, he had given way to Baruga, and had been influenced by Julian's opinion.

"He's in the group flying out to staff the Paris embassy," the hunchback said.

Wolin lifted the receiver. Telephones in the city did not work yet, but the security network was functioning more or less efficiently. He called the Ministry of Foreign Affairs.

"This is Wolin. Could you tell me when your party's flying to Paris? Today? They're at the airfield? Bad weather? No, nothing. Thank you."

"Take a car. We'll never get them on the telephone. Go to the airport and get hold of Peter Kwinto's passport. Discreetly. There's no reason to lock him up. You should be able to make it, the plane can't take off because of a snow storm."

236

After the man left the room, Wolin, deep in thought, traced out a little star. One more black mark against that clown Baruga.

21

ON THE UNEVEN surface of the road leading to the airport the wind raised whirlwinds of dry snow. In the storm, the remains of the ruined hangars were hardly visible. Soviet sentries in sheepskin jackets stood under a wooden archway bearing Stalin's portrait decorated with red tissue paper. The thin blades of the bayonets on their rifles were covered with the white dust.

The old runways were unusable. At the edge of a field of dry grass was a small hut. In front of it, the tiny, monotonously falling flakes were covering the aircraft, lonely in the flat, grim space.

It was a landscape alien to any idea of movement. Having arrived here, Peter stopped believing in the likelihood of his departure. The fact that a few hours would be enough to transfer him to some living, normal city seemed just as unreal as it had when the immensity of Eurasia was around him.

Two Soviet pilots in flat caps were drinking tea with the commandant of the airport; they sat around an iron stove with men in Polish uniforms. The passengers sat on wooden benches, occasionally exchanging a few sentences in undertones. From the expressions on their faces one could guess how tragic was the gradual fading of the hope of departure. Women in head scarfs and old hats were fidgeting nervously. Peter looked at Winter's wife, who wore a coat made out of a dyed army blanket. Her hands were shaking when she lifted the cigarette to her mouth. "She's taking it to heart," he thought. Winter, in a black clumsy coat, was looking dully at the floor. "Will he follow me everywhere until the end of my days?" Peter turned towards the window; the wind was whistling outside. Already they had been waiting for several hours, getting excited every fifteen minutes or so when the three Russians began a loud argument about the meaning of the meteorological reports.

Peter had got his seat on the plane on very short notice. He was given his passport and told to report the next day to be driven to the airfield. There was no regular communication with Paris—he couldn't delay his departure. He had just time to see his mother. "My prayers have been answered," she said. "You will be safe." "I shall return, Mother." "You won't. Don't think about me. Don't consider me. Live honestly." His cheeks were wet with her tears. Her small figure with raised hand as she waved to him grew smaller and smaller from the rear platform of the suburban train. Peter was left with a sense of betrayal. This hasty parting was the nearest, most accessible reason for feeling that if he didn't get away now he would never go.

He tried to understand what the Russians were arguing about. The pilot wanted to fly; the commandant of the airfield didn't want to let him go. The ceiling was low, visibility almost zero. He tried to follow the snatches of their conversation, but it was too liberally sprinkled with oaths, with spitting on the floor and rubbing in the spittle with their boots. The passengers were kicking their feet together, trying to warm their frozen toes. Peter went out and began to walk quickly in circles, wading through the snow. It was almost noon. The snow was getting thicker.

The door of the hut opened, the small crowd marched quickly to the aircraft. "It's clearer over Germany," somebody explained to somebody else. "Provided we're able to take off." They were carrying their scanty luggage to the plane.

The Douglas started, ploughing through the snow. Peter, pressing his face against the window, saw flat white fin-shaped squirts shooting from under the wheels. Though he was jolted and shaken, he didn't really believe they were starting. Would the pilot be able to take off blind? Mrs. Winter, who sat in front of them, cried "Joseph!" sharply. Then they were airborne.

Around them was a world of whiteness. The land, his native land, was somewhere below, covered in snow forever.

" . . . *No one expected to live to be brought to trial for his offences." The wind turned over the pages on the table. Gil tried to picture those people during the plague in Athens, which after all was a fairly unimportant event in the chronicles of the past. He was conscious of the temptation. If one could really recreate, by using the full power of the imagination, the gestures of a sorrowing Athenian woman, the expression on the face of a man looking at his dead son, the unique, inimitable shape of fingers holding a jar of wine—then time would cease to have any meaning: there would be only a great coexistence of a countless number of separate human beings, who had been and who were yet to be each communicating to the other the same complaint. And yet neither time nor the history of mankind was an illusion; to deny them was to take refuge in the inertia of defeat, to make a general law of one's own defeat. Neither will*

241

without pity, nor pity without will, was a solution. He who would be equal to the human condition must collect blood in a basin without spilling a single drop —not to prove that all knowledge was possessed already and to transform heartbreak into indifference but, on the contrary, to preserve the gifts of anger and of unbreakable faith.

Words were not what mattered. The workers in the city were silent, but the recent hunger strike, suppressed by mass arrests, had its source in their stubborn faith which was only half expressed by the protesting shout: Unfair. *Gil feared each day that he might be served, like so many other people who were regarded as unproductive units, with an order forbidding him to live in the city. To be cut off from the university library, to find himself in some godforsaken village with muddy paths, was not his only fear. Most of all he feared that, outside that cold industrial city, he would lose his last link with the mass of humanity. For good and for bad, it was there—in that mass which had learned to be silent and not only to be silent, but to repeat the prescribed slogans—that knowledge was preserved of what was just and unjust. It was they—one day, in the distant future, when they had become the real owners of the smelting works, of mines, and of the factories—who would protect with their hands the uncertain flame, and without any illusions that they were discovering absolute truth. Though he was not one of them, he was here with them.*

He went into the kitchen and made himself some tea. He drank it, reading the newspaper. He had learned recently to study it carefully. From the long speeches full of official optimism, one could deduce what danger was threatening. The most important news—for instance, the imprisonment of the Secretary General of the Party who had fallen victim to his own program of a "national road to Socialism"— was not reported. With practice, however, it was possible to get a faithful enough picture of the situation from the order in which the news items were placed, from the tone of the articles, from veiled allusions to "difficulties," and most of all from reports of the trials.

The front page was filled with the big trial of "traitors to the nation, base servants of the Anglo-American intelligence service." Gil always admired the subtlety with which trials of that kind were prepared. Dates, events, meetings were, he believed, on the whole substantially true. The skill lay in the interpretation so that, when put together, the most innocent and accidental data composed themselves into the picture of a crime. As a malicious anonymous poet once said: "From a small grain of truth a plant of lies grows; when telling a lie it's fatal to neglect the truth."

One name had a familiar ring. He raised his eyebrows. Cisovski? Joanna's friend? But he had been arrested a long time ago. When was it? Four or five years ago—he could not remember precisely. Cisovski admitted, as he should, everything he was accused of: that during the Nazi occupation he had belonged to a secret organization which took its orders from the British and Americans, that later his superior

Darevicz had given him money which originally came from London, that he had helped Darevicz to escape and sent intelligence reports to him abroad. Apart from this, his role in the trial was secondary. He got one of the lighter sentences—eight years. Gil calculated that this would mean that in three or four years' time he would be discharged if the time spent in jail prior to the trial were counted, and if his health did not fail.

Turning over the newspaper, on the third page he found an article on the development of the press. He shook his head over it. A few days before he had read on the same page a short paragraph announcing that Comrade Baruga had died of cancer. He was astounded. He had not known that that potentate had fallen as far from grace as the modest place given to his death notice seemed to indicate. Now, among those who had distinguished themselves as organizers of the press, his name was not even mentioned.

The summer sky was blue, with white clouds, and the darting flight of swallows. In the distance the sound of a brass band mixed with the rattling of streetcars. Gil put the finished pages in order. He straightened them and squared the pile with the palms of his hands. In spite of everything, a man was given a chance to get a little peace. He alloted himself a task and, while performing it, realized that it was meaningless, that it was lost among a mass of human endeavors and strivings. But when a pen hung in air and there was a problem of interpretation or syntax to solve, all those who once, long ago, had applied thought and used language were near us. You

244

touched the delicate tracings warmed by their breath, and communion with them brought peace. Who could be so conceited as to be quite sure that he knew which actions were linked up and complementary; and which would recede into futility and be forgotten, forming no part of the common heritage? But was it not better, instead, to ponder the only important question: how a man could preserve himself from the taint of sadness and indifference.